THE TALE OF THE COURT JESTER

By

Jacob Sharpe

THE TALE OF THE COURT JESTER

Dedicated to My Family

Who were there every step of the way

CONTENTS

Chapter 1

A Short Beginning to a Much Larger Adventure

Ok let's see, how do these things usually begin? Once upon a time in a faraway land, right? I guess that would be the best place to start, but really thinking about it, this story doesn't actually begin at *once upon a time*. Sure I could start it there, but to *truly* understand how I got wrapped up in this whole mess, I need to go way, *way* farther back and explain a few things first.

Now long ago, when the world was just beginning, there was this great and beautiful kingdom, and the people who lived in that kingdom were sorcerers. These sorcerers were skilled in making many fantastic things. Armor, weapons, things people had never even heard of; you name it, they could make it. And the greatest of these things they created, was a rock.

Well ok it wasn't a rock; it was actually a stone.

Let me explain.

You see one day several of the kingdom's greatest minds came together with a single stone, and together they crafted something truly marvelous. The sorcerers transformed that small, useless rock into a stone that could control time itself. Nothing like it had ever been created before. It was the sorcerers' greatest work, but you could probably guess what happened next.

You see just next to that kingdom of sorcerers was another kingdom. And the ruler of this kingdom only desired one thing: power. So when he heard about The Time Stone and the ability it possessed, the king believed that this was his chance to seize absolute control. So he went to the sorcerers and asked them if he could have the stone. The sorcerers knew about the king's evil desires however, and refused to give it to him.

The king, outraged at being denied The Time Stone, waged war against the sorcerers. The sorcerers however defeated the king before he could take the stone by force, and as punishment for what he had done, they stripped the king from his body and imprisoned his soul inside The Time Stone itself.

After that the sorcerers, realizing the dangers of the stone they had created, hid The Time Stone away so that nobody would ever find it and use it for evil.

Ok do you have all that? Because we're moving on. Oh don't worry, that legend about The Time Stone will be important later, I promise. But right now we need to get started with *my* story.

Now centuries passed and the story of The Time Stone became nothing more than a mere legend. In that time, far away, another great kingdom was created, and this kingdom was ruled by a wise and caring king named Cornelius. Everyone in this land loved and respected Cornelius, and many people believed that he was one of the greatest leaders in the world.

Still, not everything in Cornelius's kingdom was perfect. One furious, stormy night, a cloaked figure rode through the countryside on a horse carrying a small bundle of blankets. Wrapped in those blankets was a small, weak, baby boy. The cloaked figure carried the boy out to the middle of an empty field, and there he left the little child to die.

Sad and pathetic right? Do you want to know what's even more sad and pathetic? That kid who got abandoned and left to die, that kid is *me*.

My name's Sam. Well that's what everyone else calls me. I don't really know if my real parents ever gave me a name before I was abandoned. Now you may be wondering, 'if I was left to die, how exactly did I manage to survive?'

Well it just so happened that on the very same night I was abandoned another man was riding through the countryside. That man was none other than the ruler of the kingdom I mentioned earlier, Cornelius. Cornelius heard me crying and found me lying on the side of the road. He took pity on me and brought me back to his castle where he showed me to his wife, Queen Lana, and his daughter, Princess Tamina. He then did something that no one saw coming. He gave me to Princess Tamina and told her that *she* was the one who was going to raise me.

Everybody (including Princess Tamina) thought that Cornelius had lost his mind. Not only did the king of an entire kingdom take in a kid that nobody wanted and was left to die out in the wilderness, but he was also giving that kid to his own daughter for her to raise. People everywhere questioned Cornelius's sanity, but Cornelius stuck with his decision. Eventually Tamina agreed to raise me and that's when she gave me the name Sam.

So you're probably thinking that's the end of my story. I became part of the royal family, became a prince of a faraway land, and we all lived happily ever after.

Well...

Chapter 2

My Life, 13 Years Later

So you would *think* that being taken in by the royal family of an entire kingdom would automatically make me some kind of prince wouldn't you? Well that's where you're wrong. You see according to the kingdom's laws only people who were born or married into the royal family could be considered royalty, and since I was only *adopted* by the royal family, that meant I could never become a prince. If you're wondering why that law even exists, I think I remember hearing that it was created because of an incident where one of the kings died and the family dog became king instead of his son.

So if I'm not a prince, then what exactly am I? Well over the years that I lived with the royal family both Cornelius and Tamina did their best to try and find the right place for me inside the castle. They tried giving me a job like being one of the cooks or servants; but in one way or another they all ended up being a complete disaster, and we were always left right back at where we started. Eventually though, we did manage to find a job that I was actually pretty good at: being the court jester.

Now before anyone asks; yes, being the court jester is probably one of the worst jobs you could ever have. Not because it's horrible or anything, but you try explaining to people how you live in a castle, yet somehow you ended up at the bottom of the barrel in terms of social status. Being court jester doesn't earn you a lot of respect from people, but really it was the *only* thing I could actually do.

Remember how I said that when Cornelius found me I was small and weak? Well things hadn't really changed much in thirteen years. I mean I had grown, a little, but compared to other kids my age everyone looked like a giant next to me. I had long brown hair that stuck up in different places, light green eyes, and pasty white skin. I was also probably the weakest person in the entire kingdom.

When I turned thirteen I could barely lift ten pounds and even then it felt like my back was going to break. That basically ruled out all jobs that required any "physical labor." Because of that I ended up becoming the court jester for Cornelius, and for years things stayed that way; until some very strange turn of events...

It all started on the day of the celebration. That day started out just like any other.

I slept in for as long as I could like I usually did. That usually lasts until the sun creeps into my room and right into my eyes making them burn, which leads me to rolling straight off my bed. This particular day when I hit the floor it instantly woke me up because of the massive headache it gave me. When I got up my vision was all blurry from the sun shining in my eyes, and I had to hit the back of my head a couple of times until the room came back into focus. I stretched and went over to my dresser, pulled out a few of my clothes and put them on.

If you saw my clothes they might surprise you since they're just ordinary clothes. Most of the time when I tell people I'm the court jester they at first don't believe me because they expect me to be wearing some ridiculous bright and colorful outfit with bells. Thankfully though, I've never had to wear anything like that in my life. Believe me, if I did I would've died from embarrassment years ago.

After getting dressed I opened my bedroom door and started making my way down to the kitchen to get breakfast. Now even though I'm a late sleeper I had to be careful not to make any loud noises. Not because everyone else was still sleeping, but because everyone in the castle liked peace and quiet at all times during the day. That wasn't a problem for most people who were always busy doing their jobs, but when you're the court jester like me who's only job is to entertain people when there were people to entertain, it was really annoying always having to stay quiet.

As I made my way down to the kitchen I happened to notice something strange going on. Usually when I walked through the castle on regular days there would be no one in sight. However, today the hallways seem to be bustling with servants, all of them in a hurry to get where they needed to go. Everywhere I looked all the staff seem to be doing something: moving furniture, bringing in flowers, and cleaning every possible corner they could get into. I wondered what was going on, but my stomach was too busy growling for me to really stop and find out. I continued making my way down towards the kitchen all the while avoiding all the bustling people moving around the castle.

Eventually I made it down to where I wanted and opened the kitchen door. Now if someone ever came to the castle and I was put in charge of showing them around, one of the first places I would take them would be the kitchen. Actually no, I would keep them as far away from the kitchen as possible because they would just end up eating all the food and leave nothing for me. As soon as you open the door to the place you immediately smell what's cooking inside and instantly become ten times hungrier, which for somebody like me whose stomach was already growling, left me drooling.

I walked through the room saying hello to all the cooks that I knew. Over the years many of the castle's staff have come and gone, but there were still a lot of people that stayed around. I always like talking with them; it keeps me from getting bored all day. Today however, like the rest of the castle staff, everyone seemed to be in a hurry. Everywhere I looked, cooks were running around preparing food, putting things on trays, and rushing the trays out of the kitchen. I ducked in and out of people's way as they walked past, and accidently bumped into Christopher, the head chef.

Now at first glance, most people would be intimidated by Christopher. He was a big bulky man with massive meaty arms that I couldn't wrap both my hands around. He had a bald head and a sinister looking moustache that would paralyze anyone who looked at it for too long. He also had a strict disciplined attitude when it came to working. Once he started cooking, he wouldn't stop at all until

11

the food that he was preparing was cooked to perfection. But even though he looked like he could pick you up and break your back with a single arm twitch, everyone knew Christopher wouldn't hurt a fly. He always enjoyed having me around to talk to and gave me some of the left-overs from the dishes he made.

"You better watch your step Sam," Christopher said in his deep gruff voice.

"Sorry Christopher," I said, it's just that there're a lot of people here. I was just wondering if you have any spare food I could have."

"Wish I could Sam," he said turning back to what he was doing, "but I can't give you any food today, I have to save every last crumb that I have for tonight."

"Tonight?" I asked confused, "what's going on tonight?"

"No wonder they made you the court jester, that's a good one," He said chuckling. I started chuckling too, not wanting to look like an idiot in front of him even though I still had no idea what he was talking about. But thankfully Christopher kept talking. "... I still have about a hundred more meals to prepare for the celebration tonight."

I silently groaned under my breath so Christopher couldn't hear me. Now all of the strange activity that I saw happening today made sense. All the people, the moving things around, the overall busy atmosphere, it all made sense now.

"Right," I said quietly. I always hated the Annual Royal Celebration.

The Annual Royal Celebration was a party that Cornelius hosted every year and it was probably the biggest party in the entire world. Each year in the weeks leading up to the celebration, huge amounts of work went into getting everything ready. From supplies, to cleaning, to cooking, everyone inside the castle would work overtime to make sure that everything was in perfect condition for that one night. Also in those weeks, everybody in the entire village would discuss the celebration as if they actually got to go to it.

See, the only way anybody attended the celebration was if they were given an invite. Almost all of the invites that were given out were either given to the castle staff, royal families from other kingdoms, or very rich, or very important people. Because of that, this led to many people doing all sorts of crazy things to get into the celebration; from creating forgeries, posing as castle staff, scaling the castle walls, to even one person claiming to be King Cornelius' long-lost brother a couple years back. Everybody dreamed of one day going to the Royal Celebration, but I can tell you right now, it's a torture that I personally wouldn't wish upon anyone.

When people imagine the Annual Royal Celebration, they think of some elaborate exciting party, however, it's nothing like what people expect. If you want an accurate representation of what it's like, just think of the most boring time in your life. It's like that only a thousand times worse. All it is, is a bunch of royal and rich people standing around doing nothing but talking to each other all night long.

This wouldn't really be a problem, but remember I'm the court jester, so it's my job to entertain guests when they come. Unfortunately, it's impossible to entertain the type of people who show up to the celebration; they wouldn't laugh even if their life depended on it. So every year I just end up standing in a corner for most of the night being bored out of my skull. And it's that reason that every year I've managed to forget about the Annual Royal Celebration. I just hoped that tonight went by quickly.

I decided to leave Christopher to finish his work. On my way out my stomach rumbled again so I quickly grabbed an apple off one of the carts that was leaving the kitchen. I made my way through the castle eating my apple, and tried to ignore all the people who were getting in a frenzy about what seemed like little unimportant details; like whether or not that picture frame was completely straight, or if those flowers needed to be moved just a little more to the left. While I was walking I accidently bumped into Tamina walking briskly in the opposite direction.

Tamina was the daughter of Cornelius and the one to inherit the throne next. She was tall, had brown eyes, and dark black hair. Tamina was also the one who had raised me since I was first brought here by Cornelius. You think that would mean she was like my mother, but to be quiet honest she never acted very "motherly" around me and instead acted more like a big sister.

People in the kingdom said that Tamina was one of the calmest people ever, however, after living with her for thirteen years I wondered how that rumor even got started. Tamina was probably one of the most stressed-out people I ever knew. She worried over the smallest things on a daily basis, and when things went wrong she would always go into a full-out panic that took hours to calm her down from. I think her stress was caused from her knowing that one day she would have to rule an entire kingdom, and her thinking that she wouldn't be able to handle it. All I can say is, if being royalty causes you to be that stressed out, then I'm glad I'm just the court jester.

"Hey Tamina, "I said. Tamina turned around and I saw the crazed look in her eyes. Her hair was a mess, she had bloodshot eyes, and she had a bit of a twitch.

"Sorry Sam I can't talk right now. Daddy put me in charge of making sure all of the decorations are right," she said so fast that I could barely tell what she said. She took a few steps towards me, her eyes almost bulging out of her head and I had to take a few steps back so she wouldn't run into me.

"Ok, calm down Tamina. Everything's going to be fine," I said. After saying that I instantly regretted it because that really set her off.

"Fine, Fine! Everything is not fine. The kitchen is behind schedule, some of the decorations haven't arrived and the musicians aren't even here! How can you say that's fine?!" Tamina almost screamed getting right next to my face. She had a look of total fury on her face and I took several steps back just in case she snapped and started attacking me.

"Ok, ok, I'm sorry, it's just, I think you need to calm down a bit."

Tamina's face changed from total fury to calm as she straightened up and took several deep breaths. "I'm sorry Sam," she said steadying herself, "it's just that the Annual Royal Celebration only happens once a year and I want to make sure that nothing goes wrong tonight."

"Don't worry, nothing's going to happen tonight," I said. "And besides if something does go wrong, the Royal Celebration could afford to have something interesting happen for once."

Tamina smiled and chuckled a little. "Don't' let Daddy hear you say that. You know how much he loves the Royal Celebration," she said. I chuckled too as I turned around and continued on down the hall. However, while I was walking I suddenly heard Tamina scream again, "No, no that's not where that goes! Fix it, Fix it!"

I rolled my eyes and sighed. Some people never change.

I made my way out of the castle and down to the castle gardens. I walked around the many flowers and fountains outside trying to get away from all the chaos of the preparations. The gardens were always so peaceful that they were a great place to go if you needed some time alone. As I made my way around the gardens towards the front courtyard I started to hear voices. At first I couldn't make out what they were saying, but as I got closer I could tell who was talking. I poked my head around the corner and saw Stewart talking to the members of the Royal Guard.

Stewart was the head knight of Cornelius's Royal Guard. The story goes that when he was five years old he stopped a rampaging bull from running over his parents. I don't know if that was true or not, but looking at him, it would be safe to say it probably was. Stewart was described by all the women in the kingdom as the most handsome man in the world.

He definitely was the tallest man that I knew, also one of the strongest in the entire kingdom, and he was the most skilled knight in the Royal Guard. He was also the nicest person I'd ever met. Stewart was always willing to help you if you were in trouble and was someone who listened to you when you needed someone to talk to. He also had the biggest crush on Tamina. He tried to hide it from everyone, but he always did a horrible job. Watching from around the corner I could see he and the rest of the Guard were practicing for tonight.

I sat there for a while watching the guards practice. Some were dueling each other with swords, some were practicing on dummies, and others were shooting arrows at targets. Watching them practice made me think about me being a court jester. Ever since I was little I had wanted to be a knight. Watching them practice, leaving on great adventures, and seeing them help people with their problems, it made me want to be just like them.

I almost had the chance to be one. When I was eight years old I was given a test to see if I could start training to become part of the Royal Guard like all the other eight year-old-boys in the kingdom. They put me in line with the other boys who were my age (yet twice my height) and made me do several challenges to see if I was qualified to join.

Let's just say that after me not being able to lift the sword, not being able to hit the target with the bow and arrow, and after nearly decapitating someone's head, I failed my test and I wasn't able to join. After that I spent several weeks in my room sulking over how I didn't get in. I wanted so badly to be part of the Royal Guard and I knew that I would probably never get the chance again.

Eventually I got over my depression and just accepted the fact that I didn't make it. Even so, failing didn't stop me from trying to get into the Royal Guard. Every once in a while when nobody was around I would try my hand at some of the things the guards did. Most of the time it didn't end well, but I still haven't lost hope that one day I can become part of the Royal Guard just like Stewart. A boy can dream right?

"...All right men, I expect you all to be here tonight at sundown. Until then, you're free to go," I suddenly heard Stewart say.

I snapped out of my humiliating memories of the past and saw all the guard members taking their armor off and laying it down on the wooden racks. One by one all of them left to do his own thing and soon I was completely alone in the courtyard. I got up from the place that I had been watching the guards from and went over to the racks where they had laid their swords, shields, bows, and arrows. I looked at each of them, thinking about what it must have felt like using them in actual battle.

Without really thinking about what I was doing, I picked up one of the bows and grabbed one of the arrows. I fitted the arrow into the bow and aimed it at one of the targets. I pulled back, but found doing that was an extremely difficult challenge. I ended up letting go of the string and saw the arrow only fly a couple of feet before hitting the ground.

I picked up another arrow and fitted it into the bow again. This time I pulled back with all the strength I had. That was a bad idea as the string accidently slipped out of my hand and hit me in the arm. Pain shot through me as I let go of the bow and started cursing silently to myself.

"Having trouble?" a voice said behind me, causing me to jump. I spun around and saw that Stewart was standing there, watching me for who knows how long.

"Hey Stewart, hi Stewart, hey, hi, how are you doing, how long have you been standing there?" I stammered, trying to stay calm while I gripped my arm in pain.

Stewart only sighed, "What are you doing?"

"Oh, you know, just, practicing my aim," I said picking up the bow and putting it back on the wooden rack. I turned around and saw Stewart looking at me with disapproval. I tried to avoid his gaze by looking at random things on the ground, but I could still feel his stare and eventually I gave up. "What?" I said looking up at him.

"Look Sam, this's the third time this month I've caught you messing around with the Guard's equipment, and last time I caught you, you almost killed three people," Stewart said.

"But I didn't, so that's got to count for something right," I said putting on a fake smile. Stewart frowned at me, making me feel uncomfortable so I stopped. "Ok fine. I'm sorry," I said heavily, "but I'm just tired of being the stupid court jester. I just want to do something useful with my life. You know, like you guys."

Stewart stood there for a bit and I could tell he was thinking about what he was going to say. After a while he finally spoke again. "Look Sam, I like you're determination, I really do, but you're messing around with things that you shouldn't even be near. You're going to end up getting someone hurt. Or worse," he said. Stewart walked over to me and got down so that he was eye level with me. "Now I want you to promise to stop messing around with the Guard's equipment. Got it?" he said.

"But how am I..." I said starting to argue.

"Got it?" Stewart said strictly.

I sighed in defeat. "Yes," I muttered.

"Good," Stewart said getting up and leading me towards the front doors, "Now come on, the Royal Celebration's going to start soon, and you need to get ready."

"Great, can't wait," I said sarcastically rolling my eyes and thinking about the night ahead. *Tonight's going to be a long night,* I thought to myself as we walked, not knowing just how true that statement was going to be.

Chapter 3

A Boring Night gets Really, REALLY Strange

So there I was, sitting on the edge of my bed, bracing myself for what was undoubtedly going to be a complete waste of my night. While I sat I started thinking about all the different kind of ways that could get me out of going to the Royal Celebration. You may be wondering why I couldn't just skip the celebration if I hated it that much (believe me I would love nothing more) but since I was the court jester whose job was to entertain guests, an appearance was required. Lucky me.

I got up, stretched, and went over to the balcony that over-looked the front courtyard and looked down at all the chaos happening below. I saw a long line of carriages stretching all the way from the village to the front gate where guards were taking people's invitations and letting them inside. I watched people in their fancy yet incredibly bizarre-looking clothes get out of their carriages and make their way up the main steps and into the castle. I even spied some guards escorting a few people away who obviously tried to sneak their way in. Everything below was exactly like what I had seen a dozen other times in previous years, and I could tell that nothing new or exciting was going to happen this year.

I stood there for a while and watched all the party guests arrive. Finally the sun sank below the horizon and I knew that I had to get going. I wanted so desperately not to go, but I knew that if I didn't show up soon they would send somebody up to come and drag me down to the celebration. Trust me, it's happened before.

I went over and opened my door and started making my way down to the main hall, and it wasn't long before I started hearing the sounds of the celebration. Now when I say "the sounds of the celebration", I'm basically talking about the soft musical pieces that the band plays and the quiet whispers of people murmuring to each

19

other. That's what qualifies as "fun" for people at the Royal Celebration.

I rounded the corner and walked into the main hall. As expected, it was packed with tons of people standing around talking to one another. When I walked past them I caught brief snatches of what they were saying. One person was talking about how he should've brought all six horses instead of just five, one woman was stressing over how her dress looked too similar to another woman's, and one man was nervously asking people to stay five feet away from him because of something about germs.

As I walked past people I got a lot of confused stares, dirty looks, and raised eyebrows. I guess I couldn't blame them. All the people there were wearing the fanciest clothes they probably owned, and all I was wearing were my everyday clothes. Seeing me walk past, people must've thought that I was just some random kid from the village who managed to sneak his way in. I did my best to ignore people's stares as I walked past, but the way they looked at me made me feel incredibly uneasy and unwelcomed.

I managed to push my way through the crowd and into the dining room. Now when I say dining room, I don't actually mean "room" because the castle's dining room is so large it could fit ten normal-sized rooms in it and still have enough space for people to move around in. The dining room was impressive and hands down the largest room in the entire castle. Normally on a regular day the dining room would be mostly empty except for the high table where Stewart, the royal family, and I would eat our meals. However, tonight the high table had been moved to the front of the room to make space for the celebration.

As I entered the dining room I had to say I was definitely impressed and had to congratulate Tamina. Despite her over-stressed attitude towards the whole preparation this morning, she really did do a great job of decorating. It wasn't much; mostly tables with flowers on them and the occasional ice sculpture, but I felt that's what made it so great. The decorations made things feel less formal and more laid back, something I felt the Royal Celebration desperately needed. However, as I walked past people and saw their expressions I could tell that many of them were not as impressed as I was at the way the dining room looked.

I saw some people giving the decorations disapproving scowls and one person I walked past even outright told their group that the decorations were just plain horrible. I was completely speechless. All the hard work that Tamina and the staff did to put this party together, and these people only seemed concerned with picking apart every single little detail they didn't like. I knew I had to do something, I couldn't let Tamina's hard work be all for nothing.

I stopped in front of the group that had been talking and said, "Excuse me, but would it kill you guys to show just a little more respect. Tamina worked hard putting this together." As soon as I said that I instantly regretted it because the group immediately stopped their discussion and looked at me. I could tell from their expressions that they were all wondering why I was even talking to them.

"That's funny," one of the women said, "I didn't know they let *peasants* in this year, this party must be worse than we thought."

The woman emphasized the word peasant which really annoyed me so I snapped back, "Hey I'm not a peasant; I actually know the royal family."

"Really?" one of the men said in a disgusting tone, "how do *you* know the royal family?"

"Princess Tamina was the one who raised me," I said proudly. The group looked at me in disbelief and I knew that right at that moment I had them beat. But that moment ended quickly when one of them spoke again.

"Really? I didn't know Princess Tamina had a son," one of the men said.

I instantly dropped my smug attitude and shifted my eyes at the ground. "Well, actually no, I'm not her son. I'm actually... I'm actually the court jester," I said weakly. I looked up at the group and saw their shocked faces had been replaced with looks of confusion.

Then without warning the entire group all burst into a fit of laughter. "A court jester," one of the women said in-between her laughter, "He must be joking." "I don't think he is," another woman said. I sighed, feeling the humiliation from their laughter wash over me.

Eventually one by one the group calmed down. One of the men then came over to me and grabbed me by the shirt. "Listen court jester," he said in a very smug, very menacing voice. "I don't know who you think you are, but I'm the ruler of three countries, and I will not be spoken to that way by a mere *idiot*, do you understand?"

Normally I would've gotten defensive because I hated when people called me an idiot just because I was a court jester, but I was so scared that I found myself unable to do anything but stutter. "Um...But...I...Um...You...I wasn't...You see," I managed to squeak out.

"Do you understand?" he repeated. I saw the rage in the man's eyes and I could tell that he was just about to snap. I closed my eyes and braced myself for what seemed like the inevitable, but thankfully (or maybe unfortunately) the universe wanted to keep me alive that night.

"All right break it up," Stewart said walking up and prying me from the man's grip. After being released I took several deep breaths, thankful that I didn't get killed. The guy who grabbed me on the other hand had a face that looked like a mixture of annoyance and disappointment; obviously he was mad that he didn't get to hit me. "So does anyone want to explain to me what's going on?" Stewart asked.

"Nothing that concerns you," the man said giving Stewart a dirty look.

"Well since I am head of the Royal Guard, I think this actually *does* concern me," Stewart said giving the man an equally dirty look back. Stewart then dropped the tone in his voice and said through gritted teeth, "So do you care to explain why you were grabbing my friend just now?"

22

After hearing that Stewart was part of the Royal Guard the man stood there silent for a second before he turned back to the rest of the group. "Come on," he said, "let's go socialize somewhere else." The rest of the group turned around and started to leave. The man turned and gave us one last disgusted look before following them out of the dining room.

"Come on let's go be boring somewhere else," I said in a horrible imitation of the guy. I felt Stewart put his hands on my shoulders and steer me away towards the front of the dining room. "You know, maybe I should've made you promise to think about what you're going to do first before you do it." Stewart said.

"I had to say something," I said, "They were disrespecting Tamina,"

"I know that," Stewart said, "but these aren't regular people, you just can't go up and say whatever you want to them."

"You mean *I* can't say whatever I want to them," I corrected Stewart, pushing myself away from him, "Look at how they respected you." I could tell from the look on Stewart's face that he was trying to think of something that would counter my argument but he was coming up with nothing.

Eventually he just smiled and said, "Look, just don't worry about it ok. Now come on, it's time to eat." It was probably the most pathetic attempt at trying to make someone feel better ever, but I just sighed and decided to drop the subject.

Stewart led me straight to the high table at the front of the room where Tamina, Cornelius and Lana were all eating. "Hi Stewart, Hi Sam," Tamina said. Tamina was wearing her red dress which looked normal compared to what everyone else was wearing. I could tell she was much calmer then when I had bumped into her this morning, but I could also see that she was still nervous as her eyes darted around the room every once in a while. "Hello Your Highness," Stewart said nervously giving a small bow. I snickered a bit at Stewart's lack of confidence in front of Tamina. Cornelius and Lana nodded in respect to Stewart and Tamina giggled.

"Stewart, we've been friends since we were eight, you don't have to call me your highness anymore," she said.

"Oh right. Sorry Tamina," Stewart said, chuckling weakly.

Stewart and I sat down next to Tamina and some of the servants brought out some food for us.

After I had finished my meal I quietly ducked underneath the table and made my way over to the corner that I usually stood in during the celebration. I knew that I was expected to entertain people, but looking at all of them I knew that would be futile. When I got to my corner I decided to just sit and watch the party guests until the celebration ended, but that soon became incredibly dull. The only thing people were doing was standing around chatting.

There was a place in the middle of the dining room where people were supposed to dance, but nobody was actually using it. I looked over at the high table and saw that Stewart and Tamina were speaking to each other. I couldn't tell what they were saying, but from what I saw, Stewart was looking incredibly nervous which made me laugh. After a while I started to get really tired. I tried my best to keep myself awake, but after about an hour of just sitting and watching people do nothing but talk, I gave up and decided to leave.

I started to inch my way across the wall towards the nearest door. I tried to stay as quiet as I possibly could, not wanting to draw any attention to myself; I was pretty sure I wasn't allowed to leave yet. I had almost made it to the door when I suddenly saw someone walking towards me. I panicked and ducked under a nearby food table and waited, hoping the person would walk right by. But unfortunately the person stopped right in front of me. I held my breath not daring to make a sound, just praying that the person would leave soon. Eventually I saw the pair of feet in front of me turn around and walk away. I sighed in relief, thinking that I was in the clear. However, as I was getting up from under the table I accidently hit my head against it, causing the table to tip over.

Now with a normal party, the sound of a table hitting the floor would be loud, but with the party I was at, the sound was *deafening*.

The crash rang throughout the entire dining room, lasting for what felt like an eternity. Everyone immediately stopped what they were doing and I could literally feel the hundreds of eyes turn in my direction. Dead silence filled the room as I stood there, completely frozen in terror. I looked out at all the faces in the crowd and saw that everyone was staring directly at me, a look of confusion on all their faces.

I felt my cheeks turn a deep shade of red and I knew that I had to get out of the dining room, and fast. I looked around and saw the door to the main hall right behind me. Slowly I forced myself to move towards it. "Um...uh ...Sorry," I stuttered as I slowly inched my way toward the door, trying my best to ignore all the people staring at me.

When I was just a couple feet away from the door, I took one last glance around the room before bolting right out of the dining room. I pushed my way past the people who had gathered in the doorway to see what had happened and ran as fast as I could, trying to get as far away from the celebration as possible. I didn't stop running until I reached my bedroom.

I darted inside my room and slammed the door shut. I pressed my back against it and slid to the floor as I tried to calm myself down. I was breathing heavily; whether it was from the embarrassment I was feeling, or if it was from running from one end of the castle to the other, I'll never know. "Well that definitely could've gone better," I said to myself. Suddenly I heard a knock at my door. I got up and opened it and found Tamina standing there.

"Tamina, what are you doing here?" I asked. I saw that Tamina had a concerned look on her face.

"Sam I'm so sorry about what just happened back there, I came here to see if you're..."

"Don't worry I'm fine," I lied, cutting Tamina off.

"Really? Are you sure?" Tamina said, "Because if you need anything I can..."

"Tamina, I'm fine, go back and have some fun. I'm just going to call it a night and go to bed," I said.

"Oh, well ok then. Goodnight," Tamina said trying to give me a friendly smile.

"Goodnight Tamina," I said. After closing my door I pressed my ear against it and listened to Tamina walk away. Eventually I heard her footsteps die down and there was silence once again. After Tamina was gone I went over and flopped down on my bed. I didn't even bother taking any of my clothes off. I laid there for a while, pushing all thoughts out of my head and trying my best to relax. Before I knew it I felt my eyes grow heavy and I closed them, ready to get a good night's sleep.

And that's when, *IT*, happened.

There was a blinding flash of light and a huge clap of thunder that shook my whole room. I immediately woke up in terror and ended up falling out of bed, hitting the hard floor. I quickly picked myself up and ran over to the balcony to see what was going on. I gasped in disbelief!

Directly above the castle, illuminating the entire night, was a collection of white and blue lights. They seemed to be moving as if they were alive, creating all different kinds of weird patterns and shapes. I stared dumbfounded at the sky, unable to believe what I was seeing.

"What the..." I whispered. Suddenly I saw two small streaks of light come shooting out of the sky towards the ground. One of these streaks landed just on the outskirts of the village while the other hurtled deep inside the forest. When both streaks of light hit the ground, the collection of lights in the sky immediately went out and the night became dark and peaceful once again, as if nothing had happened. I stood there, completely speechless, staring; wholly unable to comprehend what I had just witnessed.

Then, without really thinking about what I was doing, I ran to my door, yanked it open, and started running through the castle, determined to figure out what I had just saw. I ran down into the main hall where people were still talking to each other, completely oblivious to what had just happened. I pushed my way past them and darted out the door and across the courtyard, up to the main

26

gate. When I got there I saw that the guards seemed to have fallen asleep, so they completely missed the lights in the sky. "Nice work guys," I whispered sarcastically to myself. I poked one of the guards awake.

"Huh, what," the guard said sleepily, his eyes half shut.

"Hey," I said, a little annoyed that the guys put in charge of protecting the kingdom had fallen asleep, "I need you to open the gate for me."

"Oh, okie dokie," the guard said stupidly as he reached over and pulled the lever. The gate slowly creaked open and I ducked underneath it and started running again. As I ran I turned around and saw that the guard had fallen asleep again, leaving the gate wide open. I whizzed through the village making my way through the streets and alleyways. After about 10 minutes I came up to the edge of the forest and stopped dead in my tracks.

The Dark Forest was a place that had gained a bad reputation over the years. People would travel there worry-free during the day, but nobody ever entered it at night. People said that there were monsters and evil spirits that haunted the forest at night and anyone who went in after dark would never come out alive again. I didn't necessarily believe all the superstitions, but that still didn't mean I was going to rush right in there and find out if the rumors were true or not.

I stared into the forest and through the trees I could see the crater where the streak of light had landed. I gulped and took a deep breath. After a brief moment of hesitation I continued forward. I slowly made my way towards the crash site, looking over my shoulder every five seconds and jumping every time a twig snapped. Looking around I saw a lot of damage. Grass and plants were brown and dried up, twigs and branches were all over the ground, and some trees had been split in half or uprooted.

Suddenly I saw something that made me stop. There was a lot of smoke around the crater so I could barely see anything. Still, through the smoke I noticed a black shadowy blob that seemed to be pushing itself up. I squinted my eyes to see what it was and after staring at it long enough, I realized that the blob was actually the outline of a person. I was completely freaked out by seeing another person in The Dark Forest at night. Were they like me and saw the streak of light and came to see what it was? Was it even a person at all—or was it the streak of light itself?

I was scared beyond all belief but against my better judgment I called out to the person. "Ummm, excuse me," I said in the most terrified voice that ever came out of my mouth. The person in the smoke immediately shot straight up. The figure whipped around in my direction. Then, faster than anything I'd ever seen before, the figure darted straight up into a tree. By this point I was beyond terrified and wanted to turn right back around and leave, but instead I continued being stupid and kept talking. "Umm hello. I'm sorry, I just came here to find out what just happ..." I never finished that sentence.

At that moment something very large hit me in the back of the head, causing me to fall to the ground in pain as my vision became blurry. I tried to get up but I suddenly felt someone grab my leg and start pulling me into the smoke. I screamed and tried to claw at the ground, but it was no use. After being pulled into the smoke I tried to get up and make a run for it, however, I found myself unable to move as my attacker started dealing wave after wave of punches and kicks to me, hitting me in every possible place on my body. I tried to get up and fight back, but every time I tried my attacker would knock me back down and continue using me as a human training dummy.

The punches and kicks seemed to go on forever, but eventually I noticed that my attacker had, for some reason, suddenly stopped hitting me. I took the opportunity to crawl my way out of the smoke. After I was in the clear I got up and saw that my attacker was slowly moving towards me. Whoever was in the smoke clearly wasn't finished with me yet and I just knew that this was the end of me, there was no going back home. I was a dead court jester. I slowly backed away and tried my best to reason with the person.

"Look, I don't know who you are, or what I did to you, but please, please don't kill me," I pleaded with my attacker, half exhausted. The figure kept moving towards me slowly, and eventually stepped out of the smoke. What I saw was something I completely didn't expect.

It was a girl. A girl, by the looks of it, about my age. She was tall and thin and was wearing a peach-colored nightdress that looked ripped in multiple places. She had dark blue eyes and long, thick, messy brown hair. Although she was a beautiful girl, she also looked like someone who shouldn't be messed with. She had a stunned look on her face. Her eyes were wide and her mouth was hanging open; and she was looking directly at me.

"Look I don't know what I did, but please, just leave me alone," I said terrified.

The mysterious girl didn't seem to hear what I said as she walked right up to me and looked me straight in the face. I closed my eyes thinking that the girl was going to start attacking me again, but after a second I realized that nothing was happening. I opened them again to see that the girl was still staring at me.

"Uh, hi?" I said, now more confused than scared.

The girl didn't respond, she just kept staring at me with the same shocked expression, like she couldn't believe what she was seeing. Several minutes past and the girl just kept looking at me, making me feel really uncomfortable. Then just when I started to think that things couldn't get any weirder, they did.

The mysterious girl suddenly grabbed my head and looked at me as if she was studying me. She turned my head from side to side and rustled my hair, all the while I heard her muttering to herself. "No it can't be...but...but everything's the same..." I heard her whisper.

"Um, I'm sorry," I said weakly "but what are you doing?"

The girl ignored my question and instead grabbed one of my arms and started jiggling it around. She then started circling me, studying every single detail of my body. I was so confused and uncomfortable by this point that I couldn't take it anymore, I had to say something.

"Umm, excuse me, but do you mind telling me who you are?" I asked her. The girl stopped what she was doing and came back around to my front side and looked me directly in the eye.

She then said something that I would never forget. Everything that had happened up to this point was nothing compared to what the mysterious girl said next. A single word that would change my life forever.

"Dad?"

Chapter 4

The Beginning of a Very Odd Journey

The night air was warm and silent. The only sounds that could be heard were the faint rustling of leaves from The Dark Forest. All was quiet and peaceful. Then in a single instant, the night sky was suddenly lit up, as two streaks of light came hurdling down towards the ground. One of these streaks landed just outside of the village, while the other streak continued to hurtle past trees and bushes as it fell deeper and deeper into the forest. Finally the light hit the ground creating a massive crater, and causing every single living thing around it to burn up and die. Smoke filled the entire area where the streak hit the earth, making anyone who would've been there unable to witness the horrific event taking place.

As soon as the streak of light hit the ground, something, *unnatural*, began to happen. At once, all the shadows around the crater suddenly sprang to life and started slithering their way towards the center of the impact. When the shadows finally reached the center of the crater, they slowly began twisting and melting themselves together, creating something truly unusual. The shadows started creating feet, arms and legs, and finally a head. If anyone had been around to witness the terrifying event, they would've described it as if the night had suddenly come alive to form itself a body.

After several minutes the shadows finally stopped moving, and there in the middle of the crater stood a man. But this man was no ordinary man. He had no features that other humans had. No nose, no mouth, no ears, nothing. Instead, the man standing there was just a pitch-black outline of a human being, his body made entirely out of the night itself.

The newly formed shadowman suddenly regained the feeling in his "body," and opened the two blank holes in his head that were supposed to be his eyes. After realizing that his body had finished reforming itself the shadowman started looking around at his surroundings; the fact that his entire body was made up of nothing but darkness and shadows didn't seem to concern him at all. "Where am I?" he said to himself in a deep, raspy, bone chilling, whisper. As he continued to look around the forest and wonder what had just happened to him, the shadowman noticed another trail of smoke rising above the trees and knew that was where he would find his answer.

He started making his way in the direction of the smoke, gliding across the ground with each step he took. As the shadowman moved through the forest the warm night air suddenly became cold and bitter, and all life seemed to be sucked out as he walked. Eventually the figure came to the spot where the smoke was rising and as he got closer he started to hear people's voices. In the still-smoking clearing a young boy and girl were speaking to each other. The boy seemed to be questioning the girl about how she got there and what was going on, and the girl seemed to be confused about where she was. The shadowman stopped walking, not wanting to go any closer. He instead hid himself behind a tree, deciding to listen to the conversation.

"What?" I said to the mysterious girl standing in front of me.

Just a few moments ago, I had gone from being stuck at the dullest party in the entire world, to being beaten up by a girl who fell out of the sky. And if that wasn't weird enough, the strange girl had suddenly decided to start calling me Dad. I really wish I could say that I've had stranger nights, but unfortunately, I can't.

It took me a while to process what the girl had said. "What?" I asked again, thinking that I'd misheard her. The mysterious girl took a step back from me and from the look in her eye I could tell she was looking me over; something about that made me really uncomfortable.

"Dad?" she said again with a less shocked and more confused voice.

32

Hearing her say Dad again made me realize that I hadn't misheard her, but that only left me more confused than I'd been before. Immediately a million different questions went off in my brain all at once and it made my head hurt. *Why did she call me Dad? Who is she? Why did she fall out of the sky? Why am I still standing here?* I needed answers and after thinking for a second about what question I should ask first, I finally settled on the biggest one that I wanted to know. "I'm sorry," I said, "but, *who are you?*"

Asking that question seemed to trigger something in the girl. She immediately spun around and started looking around the forest like she suddenly realized where she was. All the while I could hear her muttering things like, "No…That's impossible," and "but I…" The only complete sentence that I managed to catch was, "Oh man, I'm in so much trouble."

I was really freaked out by what was going on. While the mysterious girl was busy, I started inching my way backwards, hoping not to make any loud noises, preparing to make a full run for it. Before I had the chance to do anything though, the girl suddenly remembered that I was still standing there, and she snapped her head back towards me.

I immediately froze in terror. For several minutes the mysterious girl and I stared at each other in complete silence. I darted my eyes around the forest, desperately trying to find a way to escape, but before I could find one the mysterious girl decided to speak again.

"Right," she said scratching her neck nervously, "So, I guess you want an explanation, right?" *No, I want you to go back to wherever you came from and let me forget this night ever happened*, my mind thought. Those weren't the words the came out of my mouth, however.

"I'm sorry, but who are you?" I asked again.

"What? Oh right, sorry," the girl said, walking over to me. "Name's Gwen," she said, sticking her hand out, "second in command of the Royal Guard." I looked down at Gwen's hand and hesitated for a second before slowly taking it. Gwen and I both shook which, due to Gwen's incredibly strong grip, made me wince. After Gwen finally let go of my hand I started massaging it, trying my best to soothe the pain.

"Wait a minute," I suddenly said looking up at Gwen, my brain finally registering what I had just heard, "second in command of the Royal Guard?"

"Yep," Gwen said smiling, a look of pride on her face.

"But, but you're the same age as me," I said in disbelief. The pride in Gwen's face vanished and I could tell that this wasn't the reaction she was expecting. Gwen must've thought I'd be more impressed with her being part of the Royal Guard, however, I was more concerned with who she was and where she came from than what she'd accomplished.

"What's your point?" Gwen said and I could hear the annoyance in her voice.

"My point is," I said ignoring her attitude, "who in their right mind would choose a thirteen-year-old for second in command?" Gwen took a while to respond and I could tell that I had made her very uncomfortable as she avoided making any eye contact with me.

"Well, um, you see...," Gwen stuttered, almost like she was trying to figure out a way to avoid answering my question, "you did," she finally said giving me an awkward smile.

Silence followed Gwen's answered as I stood there staring blankly at her, trying to process what she had said.

"What did you say?" I asked Gwen, thinking that I'd missed something.

"Um, you were the one who made me second in command," Gwen said nervously again.

At this point I was starting to wonder if Gwen had somehow mistaken me for someone else since nothing she was saying was making any sense to me, but that still didn't explain everything, like how Gwen fell out of the sky.

"That's impossible," I finally said, realizing I should probably say something, "only the head of the Royal Guard can pick the second in command, and I'm not even part of the Royal Guard." I could tell by the way Gwen was looking she obviously knew something that I didn't and she was fighting herself over whether or not to tell me.

"Yes, right now you aren't," Gwen said almost mumbling it. "But you will be."

By now I was almost certain Gwen had confused me with someone else and I was ready to end the conversation and head back home.

"Look, I'm sorry," I started to say, "but you have got to have me confused with someone..." then I suddenly stopped dead as, out of nowhere, it finally hit me what Gwen was trying to say. All the parts that didn't make any sense, the flashing white and blue lights, her calling me Dad, everything came together as, somehow, I started to understand.

It was impossible and made no sense at all, and yet... I stood there in the middle of the forest, staring directly at Gwen, thinking about what she had said, unable to find the will to speak. *It's not possible*, I kept thinking to myself. Finally after the longest and most awkward silence I've ever been in (and that's saying something), I forced myself to speak.

"Who did you say you were again," I asked weakly.

"Um, do you want me to start over?" Gwen said nervously, trying to look as calm as possible. I was still trying to put the different pieces in place and I dreaded what I was about to hear, but silently I nodded my head for her to go on. "Right," Gwen said, rocking back and forth a little on her feet, "like I said before, my name's Gwen, and I'm, I'm your daughter from the future."

The silence that followed her statement was even longer than the last one. I stood there thinking over what she had said. I had anticipated what she was going to say, but thinking about what someone is going to say and hearing it are two completely different things. Finally after standing there for what was basically an eternity, I did the only thing that came to my mind.

"Ok," I said backing slowly away, "I'm just going to turn back around and pretend like this never happened."

"Wait I'm telling you the truth Dad," Gwen said, a look of disbelief on her face.

"Look, I don't know who you are or how you got in that streak of light, but you're not my daughter. I don't even have a daughter, ok?" I said backing up more quickly now, making sure I didn't trip over any branches or roots.

"Wait, I can prove it," she said, walking after me.

"Oh really, can you now?" I said while turning around and walking away from her, hoping she would stop following me.

"Yes, I can," Gwen shouted after me, "Your name is Sam." I stopped dead in my track, unable to believe that she knew my name. "Lucky guess," I yelled back at her as I continued walking, only a little faster this time. "You're the court jester of King Cornelius," she yelled again.

After hearing that one I got really freaked out, but still I kept calm. "That doesn't prove anything," I yelled, starting to break into a run. I thought that maybe Gwen would just give up and leave me alone, however, she seemed determined to prove she was my daughter as she yelled again. And this time it was the breaking point.

"When you were eight years old you thought it would be funny to make Tamina think she burnt her food and you accidently set the kitchen on fire."

I stopped completely dead in my tracks. I had never told anyone that story before. I had always kept it a secret because I was always afraid of what would happen if someone ever found out about it. Hearing Gwen, some strange girl who fell out of the sky, tell me my most well-kept secret was finally enough to break me down. I believed her. I slowly turned around and walked back to her, wide eyed. I studied Gwen like she did me, looking over her torn nightgown, blue eyes, and brown hair.

All the while I stuttered incoherently. "But I've...I've never told... how did you... that doesn't make any...you're my...You're my?" It didn't make any sense, it went against everything I've ever been told, it seemed impossible. Yet, here we both were. Some random girl who fell out of the sky and beat me up, had just proven that she was, in fact, my daughter. I could feel myself growing dizzy, and my vision fading out.

Gwen only gave me a weak smile. "Hi Dad," she said. That was the last thing I remembered before I blacked out.

I have to say, blacking out isn't the worst thing in the entire world, you don't even notice how long you've been out for. One second there's total darkness, the next, you're regaining all thought and feeling back in your body. The only down side to passing out is how you wake up. If you slowly wake up or if someone nudges you awake then there's probably no problem, but it is a problem if someone decides to wake you up by throwing icy cold water in your face. Guess which one happened to me?

When the water hit my face, I didn't just sit up; I stood up. The water was so cold that it froze right past my skin and all the way into my bones. I immediately jumped up and started running around, wiping the water off my face and rubbing my hands together, anything that would warm me up. Gwen meanwhile was just standing there watching me run through the forest, never breaking eye contact with me. Eventually I got warmed up enough and stopped running, but I was still soaking wet and shaking all over.

"Oh good, you're awake," Gwen said.

"Why did you do that for," I said annoyingly to her.

"Well how else was I supposed to wake you up," she said.

"Um I don't know, how about, hey Sam, can you please wake up," I said sarcastically walking back over to her. "Where did you get that water anyway?" I asked her.

"I found a little stream over there," she said pointing deeper into the forest, "I didn't have anything to carry the water with so I had to carry it in my mouth." After hearing that I gave Gwen a look of horror and disgust, realizing that not only had I been woken up by cold water, but it was cold *spit* water.

"You know what," I said "I'm going to ignore that. Right now I have other things to worry about. First off, why and how are you here?"

"Well, I kind of ended up here by accident," Gwen said scratching her head. "Accident!" I almost yelled in disbelief. "How do you end up going back in time by accident? And for that matter! How can you go back in time! Time travel is impossible."

"Really!" Gwen said sarcastically. "You just witnessed a girl *prove* to you that she is, in fact, your daughter, and yet you're trying to tell me that time travel is impossible."

I opened my mouth to argue back, but then I realized she had a point. "All right fine," I said, "I guess you're right, but still, how did you manage to travel back in time?"

I thought Gwen would immediately start going into some big long ramble about how she had managed to end up back in the past, however, Gwen just looked at me and said one thing. "The Time Stone."

I was completely caught off guard by Gwen's response. "The what?" I asked confused.

"The Time Stone," Gwen repeated. "The Time Stone?" I said, still confused, "You mean that old bedtime story about the rock that lets people control time?" For a split second I thought that maybe Gwen was just kidding, but one look at her face told me she was telling the truth. "Yes," Gwen said nodding her head.

"You're telling me," I said in disbelief, "that The Time Stone is real ...and that's how you ended up here?" I continued.

"Pretty much," Gwen said trying to smile. I stood there speechless, trying to take in what I was hearing. At one point I was about to open my mouth and ask Gwen how she managed to get her hands on a magical item that was only supposed to exist in fairy tales, but after thinking the question over in my head a couple of times, I realized how stupid it sounded and decided to drop it and not ask questions anymore and just go with it.

"Well, Ok then!" I finally said in an upbeat, cheery attitude, "It was really nice meeting you, thanks for stopping by. How about you use that Time Stone of yours to head on back home now, ok!"

I took a step back from Gwen and waited, half expecting her to pull The Time Stone out from somewhere, however, after a moment of silence I knew that something was wrong. Right away Gwen started to fidget as she darted her eyes around the forest, looking at everything except me. "Right," she said nervously, "here's the thing. I can't." Silence filled the forest as Gwen waited for me to respond.

"Wait, what do you mean you can't?" I said confused.

"Well you see, I don't actually *have* The Time Stone with me," Gwen said scratching her neck nervously.

"What do you mean you don't have The Time Stone? You just told me that you used it to get here," I said, my voice starting to rise.

"You see," Gwen said looking at the ground, "I don't have The Time Stone with me because...I broke it."

As soon as the last word left Gwen's mouth warm air suddenly grew cold and stiff. I stood there staring at her, completely speechless, unable to believe what I was hearing. Eventually I was able to open my mouth and say, "You...Broke...It," weakly.

"Uh, yes," Gwen said looking up and putting on an innocent smile.

"You broke it," I repeated, now starting to panic, "So...you have no way...of getting back."

"Uh, I guess," Gwen said dropping the fake smile.

"Which means, you're stuck here," I said.

"It looks that way," Gwen admitted nervously.

Immediately I felt lightheaded again. The whole world started spinning around me. I felt like I was going to pass out again, but Gwen seemed to have other plans. "Hey!" She said annoyingly. Gwen walked over to me and punched me hard in the left cheek.

"Ow!" I said angrily as I rubbed the place where she hit me, "What was that for?"

"No passing out on me again, Dad," She said firmly.

"Would you stop calling me Dad;" I said trying to soothe the pain in my cheek, "it's weird, ok."

"Well what else am I supposed to call you?" Gwen asked.

"Um, Sam?" I said, "You know, my name?"

"I can't call you that, you're my dad, I can't call my dad by his real name. That's weird," Gwen told me.

"Ok look," I said, "You may be my daughter in the future, but right now I don't have a daughter, so can you please just call me Sam. Please?"

Gwen thought for half a second before answering. "Nope." She said. I gritted my teeth and rolled my eyes, Gwen definitely had a snippy attitude.

"Ok, fine, call me whatever you want, I don't care," I said deciding to change the subject back to the problem at hand, "but, why did you break The Time Stone?"

"I didn't do it on purpose," Gwen said, "I told you, it was an accident."

"Accident!" I said in disbelief, "How can you break an ancient stone that's not even supposed to exist on accident?" I noticed Gwen turning her attention to other things and she started scratching her right arm.

"Look, it doesn't matter how I broke it, what matters is that we need to find a way to get me back home."

"I'm sorry," I said surprised, "But what do you mean by *we*. What do you want me to do?"

"Well, dads are supposed to help their kids out of situations like this aren't they?" Gwen said.

"Yeah I'm pretty sure getting stuck in the past isn't a situation that dads typically fix," I said sarcastically.

"But we have to find a way to get me back home to the future!" Gwen said, a hint of panic in her voice.

"Look," I told her, "I'm sorry, but unless you can find another one of those Time Stones, you're pretty much stuck here."

Saying that last sentence must've triggered something inside Gwen's mind because as soon as I said it, her whole body suddenly grew stiff and she became all wide-eyed. For the next five minutes Gwen stood there unmoving, staring off into space, almost like she was in some sort of deep trance.

"Uh, Gwen?" I asked nervously. Gwen didn't respond as she continued to stare mindlessly off into the distance. After standing there and watching her in silence for a while I started to get really worried and wondered whether or not I should go over and make sure she was still alive. However, before I had the chance to do anything, Gwen finally decided to snap out of it.

"That's it!" Gwen suddenly screamed causing me to jump a foot in the air. "What! What is?" I yelled in shock "I'm in the past!" Gwen said excitedly.

"Yes, we've already established that," I said, still freaked out by Gwen's outburst.

"No you don't understand," Gwen said walking up to me, "I broke The Time Stone in the future and now I'm in the past." I stood there staring at Gwen, trying to figure out where exactly she was going with her rambling.

"I'm sorry, I'm not following," I said.

Gwen rolled her eyes in frustration and said, "Look, I broke The Time Stone in the future and now I'm in the past. That means The Time Stone still exists; it hasn't been broken yet. All we have to do is find it and I can use it to get back home."

It took me a second to fully understand what Gwen was getting at, but after thinking over what she had said a couple of times I finally understood what Gwen was planning to do, and for one brief second I thought that we had found a solution to our problem. But that second ended before I even had the chance to smile as I suddenly realized the biggest, most important flaw in Gwen's plan.

"Um Gwen," I tried to say but Gwen wasn't listening to me. She instead was too busy talking to herself about how great her plan was. "Gwen," I said again only louder this time. Again Gwen ignored me. "GWEN!" I yelled at the top of my lungs.

Immediately Gwen stopped at looked at me. "What?" she said, somewhat annoyed.

"Yeah, I really hate to be the guy who ruins the moment," I told her, "But how are you supposed to find The Time Stone? You don't know where it is."

"Of course I do," Gwen said, "I'm from the future remember. In the future The Time Stone's already been discovered, I know exactly where it is."

"Oh right, I guess that does make sense," I said, "Well where is it then?"

Gwen answered me by saying probably the worst possible thing imaginable. "The Wasteland."

"The Wa...The Wasteland?" I said freezing in fear.

The Wasteland, or as many people referred to it as, "The place you go when you give up on life," was a place of unimaginable horror. While The Dark Forest was a place that people wouldn't travel in during night, The Wasteland was a place that nobody, *literally nobody*, would step foot in. People had said that The Wasteland was just an endless stretch of open desert that went on for miles and had no water or any signs of life in it. I could only remember hearing about one person who was brave enough to go there, and even then people said that after he did they never saw him again. Hearing Gwen say that the only way to get her back home to her future was by going through The Wasteland was absolutely terrifying to me.

"Come on let's go," Gwen said as she turned around and started walking off.

"Hold on; wait," I said running up and stopping her, "You mean to tell me that not only are you going to walk through The Dark Forest at night, but you're also going to the place that nobody has ever come back from."

"No, *I'm* not. *We* are," Gwen said smiling.

"We...we?" I said in disbelief, "what do you mean, we?"

"Well, I need your help Dad," Gwen calmly replied.

"Really," I said sarcastically, "You need my help."

"Yes," Gwen said seriously, "Now, come let's go." Gwen started walking off again and I stood there watching her, fear and dread building inside me, wondering what I should do.

42

Finally after thinking for a second I yelled, "I can't."

Gwen stopped and turned back around. "What?" she asked confused.

"I'm sorry," I said looking at the ground, "I can't go with you." I looked back up at Gwen and saw that she had a look of confusion and disappointment on her face.

"Come on Dad," Gwen said after a moment of pause and I could hear the disappointment in her voice, "I need your help." Hearing Gwen say that was surprising to me because looking at her I seriously doubted that she ever needed someone else's help, let alone mine.

"Look, I'm sorry," I said to her, "It's just that, I can't go running off on some quest to The Wasteland. This is my home, I have people who care about me here. I can't just leave them." I fell silent and waited for Gwen's response. Gwen looked at me and from the look in her eyes I could tell she was in deep thought. After a minute Gwen finally came over to me and at first I thought she was going to knock me out and drag me along with her, but what she actually did was even more surprising.

Gwen stuck her arms out almost like she was trying to hug me, but after a brief second she put them down and instead stuck out one of her hands. I took it and once again winced in pain as we shook.

"I guess this is it then," she said.

"Yeah," I said, "you still going through with this?"

"Looks like I don't have a choice," Gwen said. Gwen and I broke apart and she started walking backwards. "Well goodbye, Dad," Gwen said quietly. Gwen turned and started walking off. I stood there silently and watched her walk off into the forest. Finally after several minutes she moved through some bushes and was gone.

I immediately turned around and slowly started making my way back towards the castle. However as I did, our conversation kept popping back into my mind. With each step I took I found my-self slowing down more and more until finally I had stopped com-pletely dead in the middle of the forest. I turned around and looked

43

at the last place where I had seen Gwen and thought hard about what she was planning to do.

I looked up and saw that the sky was becoming lighter, the sun would be up soon. If I went back home now I could easily sneak back into my room and nobody would ever know what had happened; it was an easy choice. Yet as I stood there looking back and forth between the way home and the place Gwen had disappeared to and thought about my warm, comfortable bed, something kept nagging at the back of my mind, and no matter how hard I tried it wouldn't go away. *Come on Dad, I need your help.* I gritted my teeth as I, in a split second, made a decision that I knew I was probably going to regret for the rest of my life.

Spinning around, I took off in the direction that Gwen had gone. I ran through the forest, pushing past trees and bushes and ducking underneath tree branches, praying that Gwen hadn't changed directions. After about 2 minutes of running I saw her.

"Hey wait!" I yelled. Gwen immediately stopped and turned around.

"Dad?" She said surprised. I stopped in front of her, gasping for air. "Dad what are you doing here?" Gwen asked me.

"All right, you win, I'll help you," I said as I gasped for air. All of a sudden I was lifted off the ground as Gwen pulled me into a bone-crushing hug.

"Thank you, Thank you, Thank you!" Gwen screamed right into my ear. I tried to tell Gwen that she was crushing my ribcage, but Gwen's grip was so strong that she was depriving me of oxygen. Finally Gwen let me go and I collapsed to the ground gasping for air. "So what made you change your mind?" Gwen asked excitedly.

As I sat there panting I tried to think of an answer but no matter how hard I tried I couldn't think of one so I just said, "I...I really don't know."

"Work's for me!" Gwen said happily as she reached down and pulled me to my feet, causing me to grimace in pain. "Now come on, let's go," Gwen said as she walked off. I stood there for a bit trying to catch my breath and ease the pain in my side before I started following her. As I walked after Gwen I took one last look behind me, back towards my home, and wondered whether I would ever see it again.

The shadowman watched as the boy and girl walked off into the forest. "So I'm in the past," the shadowman said, "And those two are after The Time Stone." At once an idea formed inside the shadowman's head. It was a frightening and twisted idea.

"Well then, I guess they'll just have to be disappointed." The shadowman started to follow the boy and girl, but almost at once he jumped back and yelled in agony. The shadowman looked down at his foot and saw that flames had erupted from it, melting a giant hole in it. As soon as the hole had appeared it was gone, healed as the shadows that made up his body repaired it.

He looked around the forest to see what had caused the wound and he saw, to his horror, that sunlight had started to creep through the trees into the forest.

"No," he howled in frustration. The shadowman looked at the spot where the boy and girl had disappeared. He wanted so desperately to follow them, but he knew that with the sun coming up it would be too dangerous for him. The shadowman looked around the forest and saw a nearby tree that was casting a long shadow. Without even thinking twice the shadowman moved over to the tree's shadow and disappeared inside it, hoping that nightfall would come soon so that he could walk again.

Chapter 5

The Search Begins

The morning sun slowly rose over the horizon, causing light to wash over the entire kingdom. Inside the kingdom's castle Princess Tamina slept peacefully, calming down from last night's stressful events. However it wasn't long before her blissful slumber was interrupted by a knocking on her bedroom door, jarring her awake.

"Your Highness?" a guard's voice said on the other side of the door. Tamina groaned and turned over in her sleep, squeezing her eyes shut tighter. Because of the celebration last night Tamina didn't get to bed until very early in the morning, so she was extremely tired. Tamina had hoped that today she would get the chance to sleep in and relax, unfortunately it looked like she wasn't going to get her wish.

"Your Highness, it's time for you to get up," the voice called as he knocked again. Tamina rolled over in her bed and covered her head with her pillow, hoping that if she didn't respond the guard would eventually give up and go away, but no such luck.

"Your Highness?" the voice said again. At that point Tamina gave up ignoring the guard and very slowly sat up in bed.

"Yes, I'm awake. Thank you sir," she said sleepily, giving a gigantic yawn. Tamina stretched and slowly crawled out of bed. She wanted so desperately to lie back down and go right back to sleep, but Tamina was one of those people when woken up, she couldn't get back to sleep, no matter how hard she might try.

Tamina slouched her way over to her wardrobe where one of the castle's handmaidens had laid out her outfit for today. After quickly slipping it on, as well as brushing the thick, tangled black jungle she had for hair (something that took a good hour), Tamina walked over to her door and started making her way down towards the kitchen, hoping to get something to eat.

As she made her way through the castle, Tamina happened to walk right pass Sam's door and stopped for a second. Looking at the door Tamina debated on whether or not she should knock and see how Sam was doing. However, since Tamina knew that Sam loved sleeping in and practically *loathed* anyone who got him up early, she decided against it. Tamina continued on her way again and while she was walking she started thinking back to what had happened at the celebration last night.

It was the middle of the Royal Celebration and Tamina was having a conversation with Stewart. Stewart was complementing her on how well she had set up the decorations this morning when suddenly an ear-deafening crash rang through the entire dining room. Both Tamina and Stewart immediately looked over in the direction of the crash and saw Sam standing over on the opposite side of the dining room looking incredibly embarrassed, a food table tipped over at his feet. For a split-second there was complete silence as everyone stared at Sam. Then without warning Sam ran straight out the dining room door and into the main hall.

As soon as Sam had disappeared the noise in the dining room suddenly became the loudest it had ever been as everyone started discussing what had just happened. Tamina couldn't hear what anybody was saying, but she knew that with the type of people who usually attended the celebration, it wasn't anything positive. Tamina decided that she should go see whether Sam was all right or not. She got up and excused herself from the table and as she was walking out of the dining room, she caught little bits of what people were saying.

"That idiot needs to watch where he's going," She heard one person say. "This event's gone downhill from last year, I didn't know they were allowing street rats in now," another person said. Hearing people say those things made Tamina both angry and upset. Sam may not have been royalty, but he still was a hundred times more decent then any of the people at the celebration.

Tamina made her way out of the dining room and through the crowd of people in the main hall. When she finally came to Sam's bedroom door she stopped and after a moment of hesitation she knocked. Sam opened his door and Tamina could see both a hint of depression and embarrassment on his face.

"Tamina, what are you doing here?" Sam asked her.

"Sam I'm so sorry about what just happened back there, I came here to see if you're..." Tamina started to say but Sam cut her off.

"Don't worry I'm fine," he said. Looking at him Tamina seriously doubted that. Tamina had been put in charge of raising Sam since he was a baby and even though he wasn't her son, Tamina could always tell when he was upset or depressed.

"Really? Are you sure?" Tamina said, "Because if you need anything I can..." Tamina said trying to offer any help, however Sam cut her off again.

"I'm fine Tamina, go back and have some fun, I'm just going to call it a night and go to bed," Sam said to her. Tamina looked at Sam and tried to think of something to say to make him feel better, however Tamina could tell by the look in his eye that Sam just wanted to be left alone.

"Well ok then. Goodnight," Tamina said giving a small smile.

"Goodnight Tamina," Sam said closing his door.

Tamina stood there looking at Sam's closed door. Eventually she turned around and started walking back towards the celebration. When she got back to the dining room she took her seat next to Stewart again.

"How is he?" Stewart asked her.

"He's fine," Tamina said trying to give a hopeful smile. Stewart however could tell what really happened and he solemnly shook his head in understanding and didn't ask any more questions.

"Your Highness?" A voice suddenly said, causing Tamina to snap back to reality.

48

Tamina looked around and saw that while she was thinking she had managed to walk all the way down to the kitchen without even realizing it. Two of the castle's staff were coming out the kitchen door and had almost run into her.

"Princess Tamina, are you all right?" they said trying to keep the trays they were carrying steady.

"Ye...yes, I'm fine, I was just thinking and not paying attention," Tamina said. The staff members nodded and as they walked off Tamina got a delicious whiff of what they were carrying. She realized suddenly just how hungry she really was.

Tamina turned around and opened the door to the kitchen and started making her way through, being as cautious as she could possibly be; she had always been nervous when it came to walking through the kitchen ever since she had accidently set fire to it five years ago. After ducking in and out of people's way and praying that she wouldn't do something that would start another fire, Tamina managed to squeeze her way past a large crowd of people to where Christopher was standing.

"Good morning, Your Majesty," Christopher said without even taking his eyes off the dough he was kneading.

"Hello Christopher," Tamina said giving him a friendly smile. Tamina looked over Christopher's shoulder and saw a full tray of bread. From the looks of it, the bread had just come out of the oven and it was coated with warm melted butter. The buttery smell the bread was giving off was enough to make Tamina's mouth water.

"Is there something that I can do for you, Your Highness?" Christopher asked, glancing up and seeing Tamina staring at the bread.

"Ye...Yes," Tamina said as she realized her mouth was hanging open and she was drooling. "Would you mind if I took one of those loaves of bread?" she asked.

"Not at all," Christopher said reaching over and handing her one of them, "Help yourself."

Tamina took the bread. It was incredibly soft and was just hot enough that it didn't burn her hands. When Tamina took a bite of it

49

she thought it was one of the most delicious things she had ever tasted. In fact, she enjoyed it so much that she almost missed what Christopher asked her.

"... I wanted to ask you before you left; have you seen Sam at all today?" He asked.

Tamina was immediately pulled away from the warm, sweet taste of the bread back to the cold tastelessness of reality. "No, why?" she asked.

"Nothing really," Christopher said, turning back to the dough he was preparing, "it's just that he usually comes by in the morning, but I haven't seen him yet, I was wondering if it's because of last night."

"Oh," Tamina said, the warm feeling the bread gave her now starting to fade away, "You've heard."

Christopher shook his head solemnly, "word travels fast around the castle and I wanted to see how he's doing." Tamina didn't know how to answer so she just stood there, taking small bites of her now stale-tasting bread.

After Tamina finished her bread she decided to leave the kitchen before the situation became more awkward than it already was. "Well, thank you for the bread," she said starting to back away.

"My pleasure your Highness," Christopher said. "Oh, and if you see Sam, tell him I'm sorry for what happened last night."

Tamina took a moment before she answered. "I will," she said quietly.

Tamina left the kitchen, her mind on what Christopher had told her. *Sam hasn't woken up yet? He must be really upset*, Tamina thought as she made her way through the castle. As Tamina walked she did her best to try and push Sam out of her mind. However as much as she tried, she found that she just couldn't do it. The sound of the table hitting the floor and the image of Sam running out of the dining room, as well as the thought of Sam laying on his bed upstairs utterly depressed kept popping back into her head. Eventually Tamina found herself turning around and heading back in the direction of Sam's room.

50

After a short walk through the castle Tamina stopped in front of Sam's closed door. She knocked.

"Sam?" she asked. No answer. "Sam are you in there?" Tamina asked, knocking on the door again. Again there was no answer. After knocking on the door a third time and once again receiving no answer Tamina started to become slightly annoyed and began knocking harder on the door.

"Sam, come on, I just want to talk." Again there was dead silence. At that point Tamina was so annoyed that she started pounding on the door. "Sam! Sam!" Tamina said, almost on the verge of yelling. Tamina continued to pound on Sam's door until finally it burst open.

There was silence in the hallway as Tamina stood there completely motionless, her mouth agape. Tamina took one look at her raised hand which was still clenched in a fist and it finally hit her just how much noise she'd been making; she could feel her face turning red from the embarrassment. Shaking off her embarrassment, Tamina took one quick look around Sam's room and after seeing that it was empty, she quickly closed the door and sprinted away before anyone came to investigate the reason for the loud banging.

When Tamina was a good three hallways away from Sam's room, she slowed down to a walk and started thinking about what she had seen. *I wonder where Sam's at*, she thought to herself. Immediately a slight ringing started going off in Tamina's head; a small feeling of both worry and panic was building inside her. Tamina did her best to ignore that feeling as she walked off.

While Tamina made her way around the castle, she stopped to ask every person she came across whether or not they had seen Sam, and every person she met told her the exact same thing; that they hadn't seen Sam since last night's incident. With each person Tamina talked to, that prickly feeling in her head was continuing to grow more and more and Tamina was finding it very difficult to fight it off, though she did her best to remain as calm as possible.

Tamina made her way down towards the main hall and out onto the castle's grounds, all the while keeping an eye out for Sam.

She made her way around the garden she knew Sam sometimes walked through, hoping that she would find him there; but again, there was no sign of him.

Tamina's pace had picked up considerably since she had started her search and by that point she was practically sprinting as she ran towards the front courtyard. As Tamina rounded the corner she suddenly heard someone yell out in panic and she had to duck as an arrow came whizzing past her head, missing her by mere inches.

Tamina stood there in a state of utter bewilderment, wondering what had just happened.

"Guards, stand down!" A voice yelled. Tamina looked up and saw the look of absolute horror on Stewart's face as he came running up to her. From the looks of it, the Royal Guard were doing one of their daily training sessions and one of the guards had accidently shot a stray arrow.

"Princess Tamina, are you all right?!" Stewart asked anxiously.

"I'm fine I'm fine," Tamina said in a panicky tone. Tamina looked over Stewart's shoulder and saw all the guards standing at attention. She could easily tell which of the guards had shot the stray arrow because he was now trying to hide behind one of his friends.

"Guards, leave us," Stewart said. The guards saluted Stewart and started walking off. The guard who had shot the stray arrow had a look on his face that told Tamina that he knew he was in serious trouble for almost assassinating one of the royal family members.

Stewart made sure all the guards were gone before speaking to Tamina again. "Princess Tamina, are you all right?" he asked again in a worried tone. Tamina was still in shock over what happened, but she was brought back to reality when Stewart spoke to her.

"Stewart, have you seen Sam? I've been looking all over for him!" Tamina moaned, panic in her voice. Stewart took a quick step back in nervousness.

"Tamina calm down," he said dropping his formality, "now tell me what happened."

52

Tamina took a couple of deep breaths, trying to calm herself down, however, she found that very difficult to do. Finally she was able to relax enough to speak.

"Sam's gone missing, I can't find him anywhere," Tamina said, and she found herself starting to panic again.

"Ok, calm down Tamina, what do you mean Sam's gone missing?" Stewart asked reasonably.

"I've been trying to find Sam all day, but everyone I ask say they haven't seen him since last night's disaster," Tamina said.

"Don't worry Tamina," Stewart said, "everything's going to be fine, I'm sure Sam's just hiding from everyone." Tamina nodded her head, but she wasn't quite sure if Stewart was right or not.

"Look," Stewart said giving Tamina a small hopeful smile, "I'll keep a look out and ask anyone if they've seen Sam, OK." Tamina returned Stewart's smile, as she took comfort from Stewart's words. Stewart took a couple steps back before bowing to her.

"Good day M'lady," he said going back to his professional manner.

Tamina gave a small laugh. "Goodbye, Stewart," she said before turning around and heading back inside the castle. As Tamina was walking back though that feeling of panic and worry started growing again. "It's ok," Tamina said to herself trying to stay calm. "Sam's all right, he's probably just hiding, everything's going to be ok." Tamina kept talking to herself as she walked, causing people she passed to stare at her in confusion. Tamina continued to make her way through the castle until she walked past the entrance to the castle's throne room.

"Tamina, can you come here, I want to speak with you," a deep voice said. Tamina looked inside the throne room and saw her father, King Cornelius, and her mother, Queen Lana, sitting there, both busy reading request letters that people in the kingdom had sent them.

Cornelius was a tall, muscular man with a thick black beard and calm blue eyes. He had a voice that was powerful and commanding, but also gentle and compassionate. Queen Lana was described by many people as the most beautiful woman in the entire world. She was tall, slender, and almost flawless. Together both of them were well respected leaders, and many people thought they were the greatest king and queen that had ever lived.

Tamina walked in and gave a small bow in respect. "Yes, Father?" she asked. Her father looked up from the letter he was reading.

"One of the messengers was in here and said he saw you in a panic earlier today. Would you mind telling me what's wrong?" he said.

Tamina thought for a second before answering, "I've been searching for Sam," trying to use the right words.

"You've been looking for Sam?" her father said raising an eyebrow.

"Yes," Tamina said trying not to stumble on her words, "No one's seen him since last night, and I'm wondering if it's because of what happened."

Cornelius shook his head solemnly in understanding. Cornelius cared for Sam just as much as Tamina did and it pained him to see what had happened to Sam last night.

"I'm sure everything's fine Tamina, there's probably no need to..." he started to say before he was cut off.

"Ahem..." a voice said from behind. Tamina turned around to see Stewart and another guard standing at the entrance. Stewart had a look of worry on his face. The guard who was with him was looking at the ground, a look of guilt on his face.

"Stewart," Cornelius said, "What brings you here?"

"I'm sorry your Majesty," Stewart said walking into the throne room, "but I have some information I need to tell you." Stewart pushed the guard he was with in front of him. The guard looked incredibly nervous.

"Pardon me, your Majesty," he faltered, stumbling over his words, "But I believe you were looking for Sam?"

"Yes, have you seen him," Tamina said, her voice starting to speed up.

54

The guard's nervousness increased as he tried to avoid looking directly at Tamina. "Yes," he said. "You see, during the celebration last night, he came up to me and asked if I could open the gate for him and I...did," the guard said pausing on the last few words.

Tamina, Cornelius and Lana were speechless. Tamina was having trouble trying to make sense of what she just heard. Finally she spoke again.

"You...let...him...out?" she said trying to keep her heavy breathing steady.

"Yes," the guard said quietly.

"And did you see which way he went?" Tamina said, her voice becoming more menacing. The guard took a small step back before answering.

"It looked like he was headed towards the..." he paused and looked around the room almost as if he was trying to find a way to escape before continuing, "It looked like he was headed towards The Dark Forest."

Silence immediately followed the guard's last three words. Everyone in the throne room took a moment to let what they had heard sink in, and as they did everyone had a different reaction. Both Stewart and Cornelius had a look of disbelief on their faces, Lana had a look of shock as she covered her mouth, and Tamina just stood there, staring unblinkingly at the guard with a look of absolute horror. The entire throne room remained silence for several minutes as nobody was able to think of anything to say. Finally it was Tamina who was the first to "speak."

"What!" Tamina screamed, almost making everyone in the throne room go deaf. The guard took a few more steps back, afraid of what Tamina might do, even Stewart flinched at Tamina's outburst. Tamina whirled around and faced her parents.

"We have to go after him. Who knows what kind of trouble..." Tamina yelled at an incredible speed.

"Tamina, please calm down," her mother said, trying to get Tamina to relax.

55

But Tamina didn't hear her mother and kept rambling on as fast as she humanly could. "He could be hurt or worse. We got to find him right..."

"Tamina!" Cornelius boomed, in a voice even louder than Tamina's. Tamina quickly stopped talking. Her father got up and walked over to her side. "Leave us," he said to the guard.

"Yes your Majesty," he said quickly backing out of the room. As the guard passed Stewart he caught a look of disappointment in Stewart's eye, and he could tell that his time as one of the guards was over.

After the guard was gone, Cornelius turned to Tamina who was breathing heavily.

"Don't worry Tamina everything will be all right," he said comfortingly.

"All right? All right? Sam's run off because of last night and who knows what's happened to him," Tamina said.

"Now don't go making assumptions," Cornelius said, "We don't know for sure if last night caused Sam to run off."

"Why else would Sam want to leave then?" Tamina wailed.

Cornelius tried to think of an answer to her question but as hard as he thought he couldn't think of another reason why Sam would have left.

"It doesn't matter why Sam left," he said quickly changing the subject, "The only thing that matters right now is finding and bringing him back." Cornelius then turned to Stewart. "Stewart, can you put together a small search party?"

"Yes your Majesty, I'll get right on it," Stewart said standing at attention.

"Good," Cornelius said, nodding his head, "Tell the men to search the village and the outskirts of the forest. Tell them to ask everyone if they've seen Sam anywhere."

"Yes your Highness," Stewart said giving a bow before leaving the room.

56

Tamina stood there staring blankly into space, unable to believe what was happening. Suddenly she felt a gentle hand patting her shoulder. She looked up to see her mother staring down at her.

"Don't worry, dear," she said, "everything's going to be fine."

Tamina didn't know what to say. There was a feeling inside her that told her otherwise.

"Yes, Mother," she said as she walked out of the throne room, her head pointed at the ground.

Cornelius and Lana watched their daughter walk out of the room; looks of sadness on both their faces.

Aimlessly, Tamina wandered down the castle's halls in a state of depression. Her mind was thinking about all the horrible things that were probably happening to Sam right now. She tried to stop thinking about those things and to think positive, but she just couldn't do it. Every time she told herself the Royal Guard would bring Sam home safely, another image of Sam lying on the ground dying popped into her head.

Then as Tamina was walking, an idea started forming in her head. It was a small idea, but with each thought about how Sam was in trouble the idea became bigger and bigger. Then as the idea started to grow, Tamina found herself walking faster and faster. *What am I doing?* She thought to herself. *It could never work, I'm crazy for even thinking about it*, she thought, trying to stop herself from going through with it.

But no matter how much she tried to push the idea out of her head, Tamina knew exactly what she had to do. Tamina quickly darted down a side hallway, planning on doing something that she knew would probably get herself killed. But for Sam's sake, it was something she had to do.

Tamina threw open the door to the castle's stables, causing all the horses who had been sleeping to suddenly awaken and start going crazy. They whined and banged against their stalls as they desperately tried to get away from the noise that had frightened them. Tamina ignored them and made her way over to the nearest stall.

After calming the horse inside down (something that took a great deal of time) Tamina untied him, put a saddle on, and tied a large sack of food to his back. She then climbed on top of the horse's back and started walking him out of the stables. However, before she made it to the door, Stewart suddenly appeared in front of her.

"Excuse me your Majesty," Stewart said in a professional manner, "May I ask what you're doing."

Tamina rolled her eyes. "I don't have time Stewart, I'm going after Sam," she said. Tamina started walking her horse out of the stables doors again but Stewart ran in front of them and stopped her.

"I'm sorry your Highness, but I must ask for your own safety that you remain here and let us handle the situation," Stewart said.

Tamina groaned to herself, she hated when Stewart acted like this. "Stewart, we've known each other since we were eight, you don't have to act professional when you're talking to me," she said annoyingly.

Stewart looked at Tamina for a second before saying, "I'm sorry your Majesty, but I must insist…"

"Stewart!" Tamina said cutting him off.

"Ok, fine," Stewart said dropping his professional attitude, "Tamina why are you doing this?" he asked her.

"I'm going after Sam," she said.

"Why?" Stewart asked, "Your father already sent out a search party to go look for him."

"My father sent out a search party to look for him on the outskirts of The Dark Forest, but Sam may have gone deeper inside it," she said.

"What?" Stewart said in confusion, "everybody's scared of The Dark Forest, there's no way Sam would go deep in there at night."

Tamina looked at Stewart. At any other time she would've agreed with him, but right now there was a feeling inside her that

58

was telling her that Sam was deeper in the forest than what everybody thought.

"I have to go," she said, "Sam's my...friend," she stumbled on the word friend, "and I'm not leaving him out there to die."

"Tamina you can't go, you're part of the royal family. What if something bad happened to you?" Stewart said trying to get Tamina to change her mind.

Tamina only sighed, she really needed to get going; every moment she wasted was another moment Sam's life was in danger.

"If you're so concerned about me, then why don't you come?" She said to Stewart.

"What?" Stewart said, caught a little off guard by the question.

"If you think it's so dangerous, then why don't you come with me and we'll find him together," she said. Tamina waited for Stewart to answer but she could tell from his expression that he was trying to think of another excuse instead.

"I don't know Tamina, this seems really dangerous. I think it would be better if..." he started to say.

"Stewart!" Tamina said angrily, cutting him off.

"Oh all right," he said going into the stables to get a horse, "but if something happens to me when we get back, I'm never forgiving you."

Tamina couldn't help but smile at his comment. Stewart grabbed one of the horses and after putting a saddle on him, both he and Tamina rode out of the stables, Stewart in the lead. They made their way out of the castle's grounds and towards The Dark Forest, and as The Dark Forest came closer and closer Tamina prayed that she and Stewart would find Sam--and soon.

Chapter 6

We Play a Drinking Game

So there I was, in the middle of The Dark Forest, with a girl who fell out of the sky claiming to be my daughter, going on an adventure that I had no idea if I'd ever come back from. When we first started walking I had to convince Gwen that it would be safer if we got on The Dark Forest's main path. Gwen was a little resistant at first, not knowing if we should deviate from the path we were already taking, but I managed to convince her that going down the main path would be easier because we would know which direction we were going and we wouldn't end up lost. Plus, with all the rumors about the things that lurked in The Dark Forest, being off the main path made me incredibly nervous, even if it wasn't nighttime.

We made our way over to the main path and started heading in the direction that would take us directly to The Wasteland. We walked for a while, an awkward silence going between us, both of us unable to think of anything to say to each other. Finally after about ten minutes Gwen did something that was completely bizarre.

Gwen suddenly sprinted to the right of the path and, in a way I had never seen before, dashed up the side of a tree the way you would see a squirrel do and started leaping from the tree branches. I watched in amazement as Gwen swung from each branch, never losing her grip. There were a couple of times that I thought Gwen was going to fall when one of the branches she grabbed cracked, however, she would just quickly grab another one and keep swinging.

"You know," I yelled at her, "you'd better be careful."

"Calm down Dad," Gwen said laughing, "I've been doing this since I was three-years-old."

Hearing Gwen call me Dad gave me a weird feeling. I've may have gotten use to the fact that she really was my daughter, however, hearing someone the same age as you calling you Dad is...unsettling.

"Really? You've been doing that ever since you were three?" I asked her.

Gwen let go of the branch she was swinging from and landed catlike right in front of me, causing me to jump. "Yep," Gwen said getting up and brushing herself off.

"Who taught you how to swing like that?" I asked.

"I taught myself," Gwen said. "I had, I had a lot of free time," she said a little hesitantly. "Usually I would practice by running up the sides of buildings and jumping between rooftops, but I'm also pretty good at swinging around on tree branches." I stared at Gwen in amazement and from the look on her face I could tell she was enjoying how speechless I was.

Gwen and I once again walked in silence. Every once in a while one of us would quickly glance at the other person and I could tell from Gwen's expression that she and I were thinking the exact same thing; *when was the other person going to start talking again?* We walked for what seemed like hours, never saying a single word to each other. The awkward silence continue for so long that after a while I started to get used to it. Eventually the silence got the better of me and I decided to break it by asking Gwen about something that I remembered her saying. "So...," I started.

Gwen jumped a bit and looked at me, surprised to hear me speaking to her.

"What did you mean by, I'm the head of the Royal Guard?" I asked her. It was something I remembered from last night, but because of everything else that happened I had basically forgotten about it. However, having the awkward silence between us caused me to remember it and I wanted to know what she meant.

"Oh, right," she said, "I guess I should explain that." I could tell by the way Gwen was looking she was thinking hard about the best way to answer my question. "Well like I said, where...or when," she corrected herself, "I come from, you're the head of the Royal Guard, and I'm your second in command," Gwen said. I thought for a moment about that but no matter how much I tried to imagine it, I just couldn't picture myself being in the Royal Guard, let alone in charge of it.

"That's impossible." I said, "Firstly, I'm just the court jester, why would the royal family ever choose me to lead the Royal Guard. Secondly, I'm not the best person to be handling weapons. And thirdly, have you looked at me recently." I pointed to the sticks that I called arms and legs. Gwen looked at me and I could tell she wasn't disagreeing with me.

"Well yes, right now you are. But in the future you're not like, this," she said gesturing to all of me.

"Really?" I said, surprised.

"Well yeah," Gwen said, "You're taller, you actually have muscles, and your voice isn't so nasally."

I stopped for a brief moment. "Wait a minute, what do you mean my voice sounds nasally," I said offended and wondering what my voice sounded like to other people.

"Oh, nothing," Gwen said before quickly changing the subject. "Anyway, in the future you do become part of the Royal Guard and eventually you become head of it."

"Really," I said, "how did that happen?"

"It happened during The Time Stone Crusade," Gwen said.

"The Time Stone Crusade?" I said confused.

Gwen nodded her head, "that was what the expedition to find The Time Stone was called. You never really told me the full story. You just told me that in the future someone discovered The Time Stone's location and Cornelius sent out a bunch of Royal Guards to see if The Time Stone was actually real and if it was, bring it back," Gwen said.

"And what does that have to do with me?" I asked her.

"Well when Cornelius sent out the Royal Guard to find The Time Stone he asked people to volunteer for the expedition, and Stewart suggested you should go," she told me.

"Wait, Stewart said I should go?" I asked surprised. "Yeah, he did. Why?" Gwen asked. "Well it's just that, Stewart knows me. And I'm not the best person to be taken on an expedition," I said.

"Yeah, I know," Gwen said looking me over again, "but you told me that Stewart knew you wanted to be a Royal Guard member and he was willing to give you a chance. And In the end you came through for him," Gwen said.

"How did I come through for him?" I asked.

"You didn't die," Gwen said. I thought for a moment about how not dying would count as coming through for someone, but Gwen continued with her story. "Anyway you guys found The Time Stone and when you brought it back Cornelius allowed you to become part of the Royal Guard," she said. Gwen finished her story and allowed me to think it over. Having her tell me what happens to me in the future gave me the strangest sense of hope. I kept thinking about her story however it seemed like Gwen wasn't quite finished yet. "And eventually when Stewart married Tamina he made you head of the Royal Guard," she said.

Gwen's last sentence made me stop dead in the middle of the road. Gwen kept walking for a little bit before she realized that I had stopped. "What?" she asked turning around, but I couldn't hear her, I was too busy thinking over what I had just heard. Gwen walked back over to me. "What's wrong with you?" She asked. Again I ignored her as I tried to process what she had just said.

Stewart and Tamina married! I thought for a while and eventually I felt my mouth curl into a large grin. Then without warning I suddenly burst into a fit of uncontrollable laughter. For a good five minutes I did nothing but laugh at the idea of Stewart and Tamina being husband and wife.

"Are you ok, Dad?" Gwen asked with a look of concern.

"Yeah I'm fine," I said in between breaths as I breathed slowly, trying to steady myself. Eventually I calmed down enough and stopped laughing, however thinking about it still gave me a big smile.

"What was that about," Gwen asked, still with a look of concern in her eyes.

"Oh nothing, it's just that...Tamina and Stewart..." I found myself starting to laugh uncontrollably again, but so did Gwen as she came up to me and smacked me right across the face.

"Stop that!" she said.

"Sorry," I said still chuckling a bit, "It's just that...Well...It's just really funny." Gwen looked at me like I was some type of crazy person. She slowly backed away and turned around and walked off again.

We walked in silence once more. My fit of laughter had killed any type of conversation we could have possibly had. After about an hour or so I looked up at the sky to see what time it was and I could tell from the sun's position that it was around midday. This caused me to panic slightly because it was at this point that I suddenly realized two things that I'd overlooked. One; neither me nor Gwen (as far as I could tell) had any idea of what we were going to do when night finally came, and two; neither of us had any kind of supplies.

Because I ran after Gwen last night so fast I didn't think things through. So that meant I was in the middle of The Dark Forest, with a girl who fell out of the sky claiming to be my daughter, going on an adventure that I had no idea if I'd ever come back from; and to top it all off, neither of us had any food, water, or anything else that would help us survive. "Perfect," I muttered, mentally hitting myself.

As we continued walking, I kept my eye on the sun, watching it as it slowly sank in the sky, my nervousness growing more and more as it did. I was praying that Gwen knew what she was doing and that we wouldn't end up dead by tomorrow morning.

And it seemed like those prayers were answered because about a half-hour later, Gwen and I happened to walk right pass a tree that had a wooden sign nailed into it. I stopped for a second to read it and saw the words, *The Forest Inn,* cut into it. I sighed in relief as I realized that I had heard about this place before.

64

The Forest Inn was built for travelers in The Dark Forest who needed a safe place to stay for the night. Travelers like us. I was so relieved that we would have a nice place to stay for the night and have some food to eat that it took all of my energy not to shout in excitement.

Gwen had also seen the sign. However when she read it she seemed less enthusiastic then me. "We better keep moving," she said.

"Are you crazy?" I said looking at her dumbfounded.

"We got to keep moving before night falls," Gwen said, "The sooner we make it out of the forest, the better."

"We'll never make it out of the forest by nightfall," I said, "this may be our only chance to have a safe place to stay for tonight."

Gwen looked at me apprehensively. She glanced down the road and after seeing the long way we still had to go she sighed and nodded her head in agreement. Together we walked down the small dirt path that was right next to the wooden sign into the forest. After about five minutes of walking we finally came out into a clearing.

The first thing that I saw when we came into the clearing was the inn itself. It wasn't anything special looking. It was a giant wooden building with one door and a giant window on the front of it. On any other day I might have said the place looked run-down and old, but with the situation I was in the place looked incredibly inviting. Around the outside of The Forest Inn were a bunch of horses and carts tied to wooden poles. As we walked up to the inn's door my stomach rumbled and I realized just how hungry I was. Knowing that the inn could provide us with food made me even more grateful that we had found this place.

That gratefulness didn't last very long however; for as soon as we opened the inn door I knew we were in trouble. As Gwen and I walked into the inn the entire room fell silent as everyone looked up from their tables making me freeze in fear. All the customers there looked like seven-foot-tall giants who had recently been in a fight with a bear. Every single one of them had huge, vain-popping muscles, slick greasy black hair and beards, and some of them were even missing body parts.

And there Gwen and I were, a girl with a torn peach nightdress, and an incredibly skinny court jester just standing in the doorway. How bizarre it must've been to everybody in the room to look at us. All of the customers stared at us and for a split second I thought that they would get up and start attacking us, but thankfully nobody in the room seem to care about me or Gwen as they all went back to eating their food again.

Gwen and I walked up to the front counter and sat down. The bartender walked over to us and I knew from the look he was giving us he was sizing us up.

"What can I get for you?" he asked in a voice that reminded me of Christopher's, only not as warm or friendly.

"We need a room for tonight," Gwen said.

"And some food," I added.

"What do you want?" The bartender said looking us over, probably wondering why two thirteen-year-olds wanted a room.

"Just give us whatever today's special is," Gwen said. The bartender walked off and while he was gone I looked around the room. The inn was really shabby. A lot of the wood was rotten to the point that looked like it was about to break, there was a wooden chandelier on the ceiling that was only held up by a single frayed rope, and there was a horrible, lingering smell that I couldn't identify.

I noticed some of the people there were still looking at us and it made me incredibly uncomfortable. I looked over at Gwen and I could tell from her face she was remaining alert, like she was expecting one of these people to jump at us at any moment now.

The bartender came back with our food. It turned out that today's "special" was nothing more than a small turkey leg and a half a glass of water. I wasn't complaining though, I hadn't eaten since yesterday so I enjoyed every single bite of the turkey leg, even if it did taste like the meat was three weeks old. As we were eating the bartender came back with our room key.

"Here's your room key," he said holding it out. I reached out to take it but before I did the bartender yanked it back. "Hold it. I need payment upfront for the room," he said.

I almost choked on the piece of turkey I was eating, although that could've been because there was a piece of bone in my bite. Gwen also stopped chewing her food as we both realized something. We didn't have any money to pay for our meal or the room. Both Gwen and I looked at each other not saying a single word, but we were both thinking the same thing. *How are we going to get out of this?*

The bartender noticed us exchange glances.

"Well?" he asked us. We both stared at the bartender not wanting to say anything. Finally I decided that maybe if we explained our situation to him he would understand, however, looking at him I highly doubted that.

"Well, you see…" I started before the bartender suddenly grabbed my shirt and pulled me across the counter.

The entire inn grew silent as everybody watched what was happening. "What do you mean you don't have any money?" the bartender hissed menacingly.

I was shocked that the bartender knew what I was going to say, but then I realized he must have had dozens other people who tried the exact same thing as us. Thinking that didn't put any confidence in me.

"I never said…" I tried to say, but the bartender cut me off.

"Listen twig, either you and your little girlfriend cough up the money, or I get paid in enjoyment.

"Enjoyment?" I asked gulping.

"Yeah, enjoyment. From breaking your necks," the bartender said placing his hand around my throat.

I was starting to have a panic attack as I started to sweat and tried to gasp for air.

"Let him go," Gwen said. The bartender looked over at Gwen.

"Oh really, and what are you going to do if I don't sweetheart," the bartender said giving a bone chilling chuckle.

"Drop him," Gwen said narrowing her eyes. The bartender just shrugged and dropped me to the floor. Picking myself up was difficult because I was shaking all over. "Look," Gwen said, "We are headed for The Wasteland, and we really need a place to stay tonight, so is there anything you can do for us?"

"The Wasteland!" the bartender shouted looking between me and Gwen. Everybody in the inn heard the bartender and started whispering to each other, still not taking their eyes off us. The bartender leaned across the counter and got straight up in Gwen's face and whispered, "Listen sweetheart, I don't know what idiot you think I am, but if you think I'm going to believe you and that twig are headed towards The Wasteland..."

"We are," Gwen said cutting him off and leaning even closer to his face, "And we really need a place to stay, so if you'd be so kind," she said in a tone even more menacing than the bartender's.

The bartender leaned back and for a brief moment there was dead silence as he thought and everyone else held their breaths. Finally the bartender spoke again.

"You know what sweetheart? I'll give you a chance. Why don't we have a drinking game? If you or your boyfriend here win, I'll let you stay the night, free of charge," he said.

Gwen and I looked at each other. "And if we lose?" Gwen asked.

"Then I get to break both your necks," the bartender said giving an evil grin and cracking his knuckles. I thought that was a horrible deal to make and I shook my head frantically, trying to get Gwen not to agree with him.

Gwen took one looked at me then looked back at the bartender. "Deal," she said.

And so began the incredible drinking game that would determine whether Gwen and I would get a free room for tonight, or if our heads would end up on backwards. After Gwen agreed to do the drinking game the entire Inn seemed to go into a frenzy. People were moving around left and right, tables and chairs were being slid over to the sides, one of the patrons moved a giant round table to the middle of the floor and placed three stools around it, and another guy climbed up the ladder to the second floor where the drinks were kept and came down with one of the barrels.

Finally one patron got out three of the largest drinking mugs I had ever seen and placed them on the table. Gwen, the bartender and I all took our seats and one of the patrons sat the drink barrel on the table. The bartender got up off his seat and cracked opened the lid.

The first thing that hit me (and everyone else) was the horrible smell. It was the most revolting scent I had ever encountered in my entire life. Everyone in the entire Inn, including the bartender, held their noses.

"What is that?" I asked. Talking was difficult, and plugging my nose wasn't helping at all.

"Slosh," the bartender said, giving us an evil look, "It's what I use for drinking games."

"Smells disgusting," Gwen said as she tried to hold her breath.

The bartender cackled, "If you think it smells bad, just wait until you see how it looks," he said. And true to his word slosh was even more disgusting-looking than it smelled. The best way I could describe it was like gray, lumpy snow mixed with green, watery sludge. Just looking at it, I was tempted to vomit.

The bartender got a ladle out and began filling the drinks up to the brim of the mugs. All around, the inn patrons were making bets on who would finish their drink first. Some of them were also making bets on who would throw up first. After he had finished filling the mugs, the bartender sat back down and we each gripped our mug handles.

"All right, here's the rules," the bartender said, "when you finish your drink you got to flip the mug upside down and place it back on the table, first one to do it wins. Understood?" Both Gwen and I nodded our heads, just looking at the drink was making me feel queasy.

"Ready?" the bartender asked. I hesitantly nodded my head. "On three," the bartender said. All three of us gripped our mugs tighter. "One." Everyone in the Inn fell silent. "Two." I lifted the mug up to my face and got a whiff of the horrible smell. "Three."

I braced for the worst as I lifted the mug to my mouth and began chugging. The look and smell of slosh was nothing compared to how it actually tasted. It was so revolting that no amount of words could describe how nasty it tasted. With every sip I took I was more and more tempted to throw it back up. The entire inn was cheering us on, some cheering us to drink, others cheering us to throw up. I looked over at the bartender who also looked like he was having trouble swallowing his own drink.

What surprised me though was when I looked over at Gwen. She definitely looked like she was having trouble drinking the slosh, but she seemed to be doing better than me and the bartender. She was chugging faster than both of us, and although she too looked disgusted by the drink, she also had a determined look on her face. The three of us kept chugging our drinks for what seemed like forever and just when I began wondering whether or not this was ever going to end, Gwen finished her drink.

Gwen pulled her mug away from her face and the entire inn got quiet. Everyone stopped and watched Gwen. Her face was all contorted. Her lips were sealed shut, her eyes were wide, but her pupils were like dots. She was twitching and shaking all over and I wondered whether or not she was going to be sick. But slowly I saw Gwen twist her arm and even more slowly turn her mug upside down. Then suddenly she slammed her mug down on the table.

There was a brief moment of silence as everybody watched in awe. Then the entire inn exploded. Some of the people cheered, others booed, and some were mad that nobody got sick. Gwen looked at the bartender giving him a look of smugness, but it was also obvious that she was trying hard not to throw up. I spit the slosh that was still in my mouth back into my mug, glad that I didn't have to drink it anymore. The bartender sat his own mug down, shocked to see Gwen had actually finished her drink.

"Well?" Gwen said looking at the bartender. The bartender took a moment before answering.

"Time to pay up kiddies," he said twisting his mouth into a snarl.

"What!" both Gwen and I shouted. "You said if we won we get a place to stay for the night. We won," Gwen said.

"Doesn't matter what I said, I want to get paid," the bartender said getting up cracking his knuckles. I knew at that moment that we were in real trouble. Not only were we about to get our necks broken, but we had just drank slosh for nothing.

"When I say run, run," Gwen suddenly whispered in my ear.

"What," I asked her, "What do you mean by..." Suddenly Gwen chucked her mug directly at the bartender's head. The bartender wasn't expecting it so the mug hit him square in the forehead, causing him to stumble backwards.

"RUN!" Gwen yelled. Gwen grabbed my arm and nearly dragged me away. We pushed through the crowd of inn patrons who were all confused about what had just happened.

"Well don't just stand there. Get them!" the bartender yelled to the customers. There was a mad scramble as everyone in the inn started running after us.

Gwen and I ran passed the front counter and as we did Gwen grabbed one of the knives. We ran over to the ladder and started climbing up to the second floor. When we got to the top I kicked the ladder over and Gwen grabbed some of the drink barrels and started throwing them down at people.

"My drinks!" the bartender yelled. Some of the inn patrons picked the ladder back up and started climbing it. I kicked it down again, but they just picked it back up and continued climbing.

"What do we do?" I yelled at Gwen. Gwen looked at the barrels of drinks, then the people climbing the ladder and then finally she saw the chandelier.

"Quick, jump on the chandelier," she yelled at me. "What?" I yelled back at her. Gwen didn't hear me as she jump off the second floor and straight onto the wooden chandelier. I paused for a second wondering if I should jump, but then I saw that the bartender was almost at the top of the ladder. I backed up and ran as hard as I could and jumped with all my might.

I landed on the wooden chandelier, narrowly avoiding jumping on one of the candles. The chandelier shook violently as the frayed rope was having difficulty holding both of our weights. I looked over to the second floor of the Inn and saw the bartender and other patrons looking at us, trying to figure out how to get us down. "What do we do now? We're trapped," I told Gwen.

Gwen looked over the situation we were in. She looked at the people on the second floor, then at the frayed rope and then at ground below.

"I got it!" she yelled, "Start swinging the chandelier."

"What?" I squealed.

"Just do it!" she yelled back.

I did what Gwen told me to do. I started rocking back and forth, and with our combined effort the chandelier started swinging around the bar. The chandelier made creaking noises and I knew it wasn't long before the rope would snap. We continued rocking and after about ten seconds of swinging Gwen got up, and as we were swinging forward, used the knife she had grabbed to cut the fayed rope.

We instantly fell towards the ground, straight for the giant window at the front of the bar. Smashing through it, we both were thrown forward, landing on the ground hard.

"Come on run!" Gwen yelled as she picked herself up and then yanked me off the ground.

I had hurt myself when I hit the ground, so trying to run was difficult. However, when I heard the door to the inn burst open and the bartender and all the patrons come running out, I started running as fast as I could. Gwen and I ran off into The Dark Forest, never stopping and never looking back. While we ran I could hear the bartender shouting and cursing at us as we continued to run deeper and deeper into the forest

72

Chapter 7

Night Falls

By the time Tamina and Stewart had started their search it was already growing dark. Stewart had tried convincing Tamina that they should turn back and wait until morning, but no matter what he said he couldn't get her to change her mind. For half-an-hour both of them did nothing but ride along the edge of The Dark Forest, looking for anything that could help them find Sam. Eventually after enough searching the two were able to find the "anything" that they were hoping for as Tamina rode into a small clearing and gasped.

"Stewart! Come look at this!" she yelled. There was the sound of hooves pounding the ground and Stewart came bursting into the clearing, thinking that something had happened to her.

"Tamina what..." Stewart started before he stopped dead.

Tamina was standing on the edge of a crater. The crater itself wasn't very big, but whatever had caused it did some pretty large damage. All around plants were shriveled up, entire trees had been uprooted, and Tamina could smell the faint scent of smoke. Tamina looked around the area, unable to believe what she saw.

"What happened here?" She asked.

"I don't know," Stewart answered bewildered. Both of them dismounted and started looking around. "I don't like this," Stewart said as he examined some of the dead plants. Just then both of their horses whined as they tried to run away. Tamina quickly grabbed both horses' reins to keep them from escaping.

"What's wrong with them?" She asked, trying to calm them down.

"Something weird happened here," Stewart said, "I think they can sense it."

"Do you think this has anything to do with Sam?" Tamina asked.

"I'm not sure," Stewart said, "but if it does, Sam's probably..." Stewart stopped as he realized what he was saying. He turned around and saw the look of horror on Tamina's face. "But uh, you know what, I wouldn't even worry about it," Stewart said trying to keep Tamina from having a panic attack, "This probably doesn't even have anything to do with Sam."

"Uh, I wouldn't be too sure about that," Tamina said looking down.

On the ground right beneath their feet were freshly made footprints. Some of them looked like they had been made by someone who was barefoot, but others looked like they had been made by someone with boots on. "Are those..?" Tamina asked. Stewart bent down and started measuring them. The footprints were too big to be Sam's but the boot prints seemed to match the size of his foot.

"I think they are," Stewart said. Tamina felt her heart stop.

"What was Sam doing here?" she asked. Stewart continued to look over the footprints and as he did he saw more of them leading deeper into the forest.

"Come on, let's go find your dad," he said getting up.

"Wait! We're giving up?" Tamina asked.

"No, we're going back and telling your dad about this," Stewart said, climbing onto his horse.

"So, we're giving up," Tamina said annoyingly. Stewart silently groaned.

"Tamina, something weird is going on here. We need to go tell your dad," he said.

"Fine," Tamina said getting on her horse, "you go back and tell dad and I'll follow those footprints."

Tamina steered her horse around and started riding off into the forest. "What! No!" Stewart yelled in shock. Stewart whirled his horse around and rode right in front of Tamina, blocking her. "Tamina you can't," he said.

"Why not?" Tamina asked stubbornly.

"First, you can't go riding in The Dark Forest at night. It's dangerous. Second, we don't even know if those are Sam's footprints." Stewart said.

"But you said they were," Tamina said, trying to go around Stewart.

"I could be wrong. I've been wrong before," Stewart said.

Tamina didn't buy it. She knew those were Sam's footprints. She didn't exactly know how she knew, it was just some kind of feeling inside her, but she definitely knew they were Sam's.

"Look, those footprints are our only clue to finding him. Now are you going to help me or not?" Tamina asked sternly.

Stewart knew he was fighting a battle he couldn't win. He desperately tried to think of something that could stop Tamina, but everything he thought of he knew wouldn't work. Eventually, he sighed in defeat.

"Fine," he said, getting out of Tamina's way, "but you better hope you're right."

"Don't worry, I am," Tamina said smiling. Stewart led the way again as he and Tamina rode into The Dark Forest.

A few miles away, darkness washed over the forest, and a shadow melted right out of one of the trees and began twisting itself into human form. When the shadowman had fully reconstructed his body he looked around at his surroundings to see how far he had come. When the boy and girl had run off into the forest the shadowman had tried to follow them, however, since it was daytime he couldn't walk out in the open and was forced to move between the shadows the trees created. He had lost sight of them when he reached the forest's main path. However, now that it was night out, he was free from the chains of sunlight and could move around as he pleased.

The first thing that the shadowman did was snap his fingers together. With that one snap the shadows around him once again started moving. They all slithered together and started twisting and morphing themselves into the shape of a gigantic horse. The horse sprang to life and let out an ear piecing whine as it reared up on its hind legs. The shadowman climbed up on the horse, and as soon as he sat down the horse took off. The dark rider blazed down the main path, knowing that it would lead him directly to the edge of The Wasteland. Eventually after riding for a few hours, something caught his attention.

Off to the right side of the road there was a small path that led into the forest. There seemed to be light coming from somewhere inside. The shadowman rode up to the pathway and saw nailed to a tree a wooden sign that said, *The Forest Inn*. After reading the sign the shadowman started going down the side path and after a few minutes he came to the clearing where the inn was.

The first thing the shadowman noticed was the poor shape the inn was in. There was a big broken window on the front of the inn, and from the smell of burnt wood, it was obvious there had been a fire recently. As the shadowman got closer to the inn he saw that the inside was in rough shape too. There were tables and chairs thrown everywhere and it looked like the fire had burnt a good portion of the interior. He also noticed a bunch of savage-looking men standing around talking to each other. None of this interested the shadowman however, and he was about to turn around and continue on his way when one of the men wandering within said something that made him stop. "Stupid kids destroyed my inn."

Inside the inn the bartender was looking dimly over the damage the boy and girl caused. Many of his drink barrels had been smashed and the chandelier that crashed through the window had started a fire that burnt a good portion of the building. Overall the bartender's Inn was almost completely destroyed and the people who were responsible had gotten away. The bartender sat in near darkness. He wanted so desperately to chase after the two who did this to him and make them pay, but since the two had run off before he could catch them, all he could do now was just curse at them and the loitering customers who had refused to chase them.

The bartender tried to clean the mess up that had been made. He put the tables and chairs back into their proper places and wiped the drinks that had been spilled. Some of the inn's customers who didn't leave after the big incident also tried to help out. While they were cleaning, there was an ear shattering bang as the inn door was thrown open. The bartender whirled around, angry that somebody would throw open the door that hard when his inn was already almost destroyed, but as soon as he saw the person standing in the doorway, he took a step back in fear. Some of the inn patrons gasped in horror.

Standing in the doorway was the dark outline of an incredibly tall man. Or at least that was what the bartender thought until the man stepped inside and the bartender realized that it wasn't a dark outline, but just the man himself. The shadowman stood there in the middle of the inn, looking around at all the people in the room. Everyone in the inn stared at the man in shock, no one had ever seen anything like him before.

The shadowman saw the bartender standing there, staring at him, and slowly walked over to him. "Are you the owner," the shadowman said in his cold raspy voice.

The bartender looked at the shadowman utterly petrified. "Ye...Yeah, what do you want?" he asked trying to appear tough, but instead sounded intimidated.

The shadowman thought for a moment before answering, "A drink," he said.

The bartender couldn't believe what he'd heard. He tried to think of an answer but all he could say was, "We're all out."

"What about that?" the shadowman said, turning his gaze towards one of the only barrels that hadn't been destroyed, the barrel of slosh. The bartender looked over at the barrel and then slowly went over, picked up one of the mugs that had fallen to the floor and dipped out some slosh. While he was pouring out the drink the bartender never took his eyes off of the shadowman, unable to believe what he was witnessing. He then went back over and hesitantly stuck out his arm.

The shadowman took the drink and when he grabbed the mug the bartender felt the icy chill in the shadowman's touch. The shadowman lifted the mug to his face and placed it on his nonexistent mouth and began to drink. Everybody in the inn watched in horror as the shadowman stood there drinking the slosh without even flinching.

When he had finished he threw the mug to the floor. By that time the bartender was completely terrified and wasn't even trying to hide it. "What are you?" he asked almost in a whimper.

The shadowman looked at him with the two holes that he had for eyes and the bartender froze in fear. "I'm just a simple traveler, that's all," the shadowman said innocently, "however, while I was walking by your lovely place I happened to overhear you mention what happened here."

"Yeah, so?" the bartender said.

"So, I happen to know the two who did this to your bar, and I was wondering if you would be so kind as to point me in the direction they were headed." The voice was deliberately civil, but the bartender and customers listening had no doubt that violence was imminent if the horrifying dark figure didn't get what he wanted.

The bartender hesitated before answering. "They, they ran off into the forest. Looked like they were headed southwest," he managed to squeak out. The shadowman thought for a moment before he walked over to the bartender. The bartender flinched as he took a step back. He wondered what was going to happen to him, but the shadowman just looked at him and said, "You've done me a great service. I thank you." The shadowman then turned right around, walked to the inn door, and threw it open again.

"Who are you?" the bartender asked again feebly. The shadowman stopped in the doorway and turned around to face the bartender.

"You may call me Lord Tharon," he said. And with that, he darted out of the inn.

Chapter 8

A Night in the Forest

We ran. That's all Gwen and I did for the longest time. We didn't know where we were or where we were going; we didn't even know if we were still being chased. All we knew was we had to get as far away from that inn as possible.

As soon as we had lost sight of the few men chasing us Gwen darted straight up into the trees and started swinging from the branches again, and I had to run faster just to keep up with her. Finally, after what felt like an eternity, Gwen jumped down and stopped. While I was running my back started to feel like it was about to give out and when I finally caught up to her it did. I fell to the ground, gasping for air. "I think we've lost them," Gwen said, looking back at where we came.

"Yeah, I'm pretty sure we lost them a couple days ago," I said between deep breaths.

"Well, I just wanted to be on the safe side," Gwen said, walking over to me.

I stared at Gwen in disbelief, "Safe? Safe? You call being in The Dark Forest at night safe?" I asked.

"Well at least it's better than getting our necks broken," Gwen said.

"You're right," I said sarcastically, standing up, "getting mauled to death is *definitely* better than having someone rip my head off."

"Oh man up Dad we'll be fine," Gwen said rolling her eyes.

"Fine? Fine?" I said practically shouting, "Didn't you hear me. We are in The Dark Forest, *at night*. Do you know the kinds of things that live in here that would love nothing more than to rip out our insides and use our bones as toothpicks?"

Just then there was a rustling noise inside the bushes. Terror shot through me as I spun around to face where the noise was coming from. The rustling noise became louder and louder as whatever was in the trees was getting closer. I took a few steps back, preparing to flee, however, right when I was about to make a full run for it, a squirrel came darting out of the bushes and ran straight into the tree.

Gwen gave me a pathetic look. "Watch out! It has a taste for human flesh!" she said sarcastically.

"Ha, ha, very funny," I said dryly.

"Relax Dad," Gwen said confidently, grabbing and putting me in a choke-hold, "remember we're the best the Royal Guard has to offer, we know what we're doing."

"Uh, yeah, you may know what you're doing," I said prying Gwen off of me, "but I'm still the court jester here, I'm not qualified for any of this."

Gwen shrugged, "I guess it doesn't matter," she said, "I'm still second in command of the Royal Guard, survival's the second thing they teach you when you join."

"Really? What's the first?" I asked. "How to not stab yourself when picking up a sword," she replied. I thought that over in my head as Gwen continued.

"All right first things first; if we're going to survive tonight we're going to need the essentials: food, water, and fire. Dad, you go over there and try to find anything that can be used to start a fire. I'll try to find the food and water," she said.

I snapped back to reality. "Wait a minute, you want me to go looking for wood, *alone*?" I asked nervously.

"What, you scared?" Gwen asked raising an eyebrow.

"Yes," I said nodding my head vigorously. Gwen only rolled her eyes as she walked up to me, spun me around, and pushed me in the direction I was supposed to go.

"Don't worry Dad, you'll be fine," she said. As I walked off Gwen called after me, "Oh, and if you're not back in ten minutes, I'm going to assume you're dead and come looking for your body," she said sarcastically.

"Gee, thanks for that comforting thought," I yelled back dryly.

80

I walked off into the forest, picking up any sticks I thought could be used to make a good fire, doing my best not to wander too far from Gwen; I was already nervous, the last thing I wanted to do was get lost. At first everything went smoothly, but after a couple a minutes I started hearing a strange rustling noise behind me. I turned around to see what it was but didn't see anything, so I went back to picking up sticks again. After another minute of searching I heard the rustling noise behind me again. I whirled around trying to find where the noise was coming from, hoping beyond hope that it was just another squirrel.

As I looked the rustling kept getting louder and louder. I tried to stay calm as I slowly started to back up, however, as the rustling continued I panicked and dropped the sticks I was holding. I tried to make a run for it but I accidently caught my foot on a root in the ground and tripped. I stumbled to get back up and run, but by then it was too late as I realized that whatever was making the rustling sound wasn't in the bushes. It was in the trees above me! I braced myself for the worst as the creature got ready to attack.

Suddenly there was a seething blaze of light and I had to cover my eyes. There was a loud thud as I heard the creature hit the ground and the light immediately died away. I uncovered my eyes and saw, to my amazement, that the pile of sticks I had been collecting was now suddenly on fire. What amazed me even more was the fact that the fire was bigger than anything that those tiny sticks could've produced.

The flame itself was about three feet high and as I got nearer, it felt hotter than any other fire I'd been close to in my life. I stared at the fire in bewilderment, unable to make sense of what'd just happened, however as I looked closer at the fire I realized that it wasn't really a fire at all.

Inside the flame I could see a faint yet unmistakable outline of a creature moving around. The creature seemed to blend perfectly into the fire, and at first I thought I was just seeing things. But the unusual way the flames were moving only confirmed that there was some type of animal inside. I stared at the fire, confused about what I should do.

I debated whether or not I should make a run for it. The creature seemed too small to be dangerous, but then I remembered that looks could be deceiving. I saw the creature moving around and I knew that it was regaining consciousness. I decided to not take any chances and leave before it fully came back around. I got up and started to walk off, however there was a sudden "SQUAK!" right behind me and I stopped. I turned around and clearly saw what the creature in the fire really was.

It was a phoenix.

Or at least, from the looks of it, a baby phoenix. The small bird was about six inches tall and look very similar to a falcon. However instead of normal feathers covering its body, the tiny bird was covered in bright red-and-gold flames. It had a long flowing tail and the two sparkling golden eyes, and although the bird was small, its flaming feathers lit up the entire part of the forest we were in.

I stared at the bird in pure fascination, unable to believe what I was seeing. I had heard of phoenixes from stories Tamina use to read to me when I was little, but the legendary birds were always thought to be just that, legends. This bird was staring directly up at me. I stood there unable to think of anything to do. I couldn't tell whether the bird was friendly or not and I was afraid that if I made any sudden movements it was going to start attacking me. I decided that maybe if I moved slowly I could get far enough away from it without it hurting me.

I took a small step backwards and to my disbelief the phoenix hopped one step forward towards me. I stopped and stared at the phoenix and the small bird stood there staring back. After waiting for a minute I decided to try again, only this time I took two steps backwards. To my amazement the small bird hopped two steps forward.

I stopped again and stood there, afraid of making any more sudden movements, wondering what I was going to do next. Everything I did the bird copied. I was thinking about how I was supposed

82

to get away from it when, to my bewilderment, the baby phoenix suddenly unfolded its wings and started flapping them.

The tiny bird flew up to about eye level and started flying towards me. I could tell by the way the tiny bird was flying it had very little flight experience. The bird would be flying only for it to drop a couple of inches and then suddenly flip over in midair before returning to its original height. The bird continue to fly closer and as it got nearer the air around me became extremely hot. Eventually the small bird flew right next to my face and I wondered what it was going to do, but I was surprised to see that instead of lighting me on fire it started flying around my head chirping happily.

"Um, what are you doing?" I asked the bird. The bird continued to fly around my head chirping madly. I was beginning to wonder if the baby phoenix was crazy when it suddenly sat down on my shoulder and started nuzzling me. Not only did this cause a sharp pain to go through my right cheek but it also caught my clothes on fire.

"GAH!" I yelled jumping back, causing the phoenix to plummet to the ground. I quickly put the fire out on my shoulder then started rubbing my cheek trying to soothe the pain. Eventually after the pain had ceased I looked down to see that the baby phoenix had hit its head on the ground and was now hobbling around in a state of confusion. I got down on my knees and asked the bird, "What was that for?" The bird shook his head and looked up at me. For one second I thought from the way the bird was eyeing me it was going to start attacking, but then it did something even more surprising.

The baby phoenix started flapping its wings again and went back to flying around my head chirping happily. I was completely baffled by how the phoenix was acting around me. I had to duck a couple of times to avoid being set on fire again. "Come on, get out of here," I said trying to swat the bird away. The phoenix dodged my swats and kept zooming around my head.

"Come on, isn't your mom missing you or something," I said. The tiny bird suddenly stopped in front of my face and started chirping wildly. I was confused at why the small bird was suddenly acting crazier than before, but then something hit me. "Wait a minute," I said, "you don't think..." The baby phoenix once again tried to get close and start nuzzling me, but I quickly backed up. "Well I guess that answers my question," I said out loud. The baby bird kept whizzing past my head joyfully while I thought about the situation I was now stuck in.

If I tried to leave the bird would just follow me. However, taking the bird along would probably be just as bad of an idea. Gwen was already crazy as it was, I didn't need a mystical bird following me around all the time, threatening to set me on fire. I could try to out-run it, but I didn't know how fast a phoenix could fly and I knew, looking at the bird, it would be pointless. That bird would follow me to the ends of the earth.

I knew I had to come to a decision and fast, otherwise if I didn't get back soon, Gwen was going to think I was dead. I looked down at the baby phoenix who had landed back on the ground and was now staring at me. I peered around the forest trying to see if I could find the phoenix's real mom, however, the phoenix was the only creature in sight. I looked back at the little bird and saw it still staring at me with its large, round, golden eyes. I sighed to myself and finally decided what I was going to do.

"Gwen! Gwen!" I shouted, "I got the fire wood you wanted." I wandered through the forest, trying to remember where I was supposed to meet Gwen. I had decided not to leave the baby phoenix in the forest alone and instead decided to take it along with me. Because I couldn't physically touch the baby phoenix, I was forced to find a stick that the little bird could ride on. I had to hold the stick out at arm's length not only because getting near the bird was incredibly dangerous, but also because when the bird had jumped on the stick he had lit the end of it on fire and it was still burning.

I walked around for a while yelling Gwen's name until she finally answered. "Oh good, you've been gone 8 minutes and 46 seconds, I was starting to worry I'd have to come in and get your body," she said chuckling.

84

"Wait, you were actually counting?" I said, amazed but also a bit freaked out that Gwen was actually keeping track at how long I was gone.

"Well I was wondering why it was taking you so long to get just a couple of sticks," she said.

"Well I had a little problem that kind of dropped on me," I said looking at the baby phoenix and chuckling.

"What are you talking about D...?" Gwen started to say before I came out from behind a tree.

Both Gwen and the baby phoenix locked eyes with each other. As soon as the bird saw Gwen his round eyes became slits and he suddenly propelled himself from the branch I was carrying him on straight towards Gwen.

"AHHH!" Gwen screamed as she ducked as the phoenix came swooping by her. The tiny bird flew around Gwen trying to attack her, causing Gwen to pick up a large stick and start swinging at it.

"Hey stop it...*you*!" I yelled as I dropped the sticks I was carrying and ran over to Gwen to try and shoo the bird away. The baby phoenix dodged my arms and continued trying to peck Gwen, believing that Gwen was some sort of threat.

"Get...this...bird...off...me!" Gwen yelled still trying to knock the bird out of the air.

"Stop it, Stop it!" I yelled at the bird but to no avail. I was running out of ideas on what to do so finally I yelled the first thing that popped into my head. "Pipsqueak, Stop!"

The tiny bird suddenly froze in midair. It took one look at me then flew to the nearest tree and sat down on one of its branches, setting it ablaze. I ran over to Gwen and helped her up. "It's ok, she's my... friend," I said to the bird.

"SQUAK," the phoenix said, still eyeing Gwen suspiciously.

"What is that thing?" Gwen said, breathing heavily as she got up.

"It's a baby phoenix," I said looking over at the bird on the branch, "I guess his name's Pipsqueak." I don't know what I was thinking when I came up with that name, I just said the first thing

85

that came to my mind; It seemed to fit with the small bird, and the phoenix didn't seem to mind that name.

"Ok, and what's it doing here?" Gwen said annoyingly, seemingly dismissing the fact that the bird I brought back was a mythical creature.

"Ok here's a funny story," I said laughing a little, "Pipsqueak thinks, I'm his mother." I thought (or at the very least hoped) that Gwen would start laughing along with me, but apparently that was too much to ask for because she didn't even give me a chuckle. Instead Gwen took one look at me and then one look at Pipsqueak who was still eyeing her.

"No," Gwen said, realizing what I was going to tell her.

"Oh come on, why not?" I asked Gwen. "How about, that bird has it out for me?" Gwen said.

"Oh come on," I said, "he was just scared about seeing another person that's all; he's harmless."

"He almost burnt me to a crisp," Gwen practically yelled.

"Ok, mostly harmless," I said. Gwen rolled her eyes, "Look we already have enough to deal with, the last thing we need is your, *baby,* here causing trouble," she said. Gwen walked past me towards the branch Pipsqueak was on. However as soon as Gwen was about five feet away, Pipsqueak flared his wings and screeched at her. Gwen immediately jumped back and retreated.

"On second thought," she said, "I've always wanted a little brother." After hearing Gwen say that I had to restrain myself to keep me from bursting out laughing.

As Gwen turned around walked past I said, "Oh don't worry Gwen. You'll always be my favorite child. No one can ever replace you," In the most innocent voice I could do.

"Oh shut up Mom," Gwen said, picking one of my sticks off the ground and chucking it at me. At that point I couldn't help but laugh as Gwen gave me an annoyed look and started to prepare the fire.

Getting a fire started was easier than I'd expected, but that was mainly because of Pipsqueak. After Gwen had finished arranging the sticks I had found in a nice, neat pile, she started looking around for something she could use to light them, but before she could find anything Pipsqueak had swooped down and sat on one of the sticks which started a warm, blazing fire.

"Showoff," Gwen said, giving the bird a dirty look, "He was probably trying to set me on fire again and just missed."

I chuckled a bit, "You know what? You two are siblings," I said.

"Oh shut up," Gwen said, giving me another annoyed look.

"No I'm serious, I can defiantly see the family resemblance," I said, "Look, both of you are hot-headed." I had to duck as Gwen threw another stick at me. "All right, All right, I'll stop," I said, almost going into another hysterical laughing fit. After calming down I tried to think of something else to talk about before there would be another awkward silence between us. "So, how's being second in command?" It was probably the stupidest question, but it was the only one I could think of at the moment and luckily Gwen didn't seem to mind being asked.

"It's fine. A lot of hard work and responsibility though," she said.

"How much work?" I asked, curious to know what it was like being one of the people in charge of an entire army. "A lot," Gwen quietly said.

"Oh," I said, seeing Gwen growing a little bit uncomfortable, "So, how long have you've been second in command?" I asked, trying to keep the conversation going.

"Actually, I just got promoted two weeks ago," Gwen said.

"Wait, you've only been second in command for two weeks," I said shocked.

"Yeah, so what?" Gwen asked looking up, and I could see a tiny hint of anger in her eye.

"Well it's just that, do you really think you can…" I started to say before Gwen cut me off.

"Why are you worried? I've been training almost my whole life to be a part of the Royal Guard. So what if I've only been second in command for two weeks. I still know what I'm doing, I've got everything under control," Gwen said in a voice that started out calm but became more agitated as she kept talking.

"Oh yeah, you've got everything under control." I said chuckling, trying to lighten the mood. "Says the girl who somehow broke an ancient mystical artifact and destroyed an entire inn, all in two days."

I meant for the comment to be a simple joke, but it was obvious from the way Gwen was staring into the fire, I'd had hit a nerve. Gwen suddenly got up and did the fakest yawn I had ever heard. "Well, I'm going to bed now. Dad, you take the first watch. If you see anything wake me up." And with that Gwen walked over to the tree that was the farthest away from Pipsqueak and laid down.

"Gwen," I said trying to get her to answer. Gwen was facing away from me but it was obvious that she was still awake from the way she was fidgeting. After a while I gave up and instead started stroking the fire, wondering what I had said wrong to her.

It hadn't been that long since Gwen had "fallen" asleep. By that time Gwen had actually gone to sleep and I could hear her snoring rather loudly. Pipsqueak had also gone to bed, and I was surprised to see that when the baby phoenix had fallen asleep, he was no longer made out of fire, but instead looked like a normal bird with red and gold wings.

I had stopped tending the fire and now it was little more than a few dimly lit ashes. Even though Gwen had put me in charge of the first watch I was finding it incredibly difficult to stay awake. A lot of the time I caught myself dozing off. I hadn't gotten any sleep since the night before the Royal Celebration and that was two days ago, so it was a challenge trying to force myself to stay awake.

I thought about waking Gwen up to change shifts but I didn't know how much time had passed since she had fallen asleep and I didn't want to risk waking her up. As time passed I found myself losing my battle to stay awake as I drifted more and more to sleep. Finally just when I was about to close my eyes and take what I thought was a well-deserved nap, something happened that startled me awake.

It was the sound of a twig snapping. I sat straight up, a sense of panic shooting through me. At first I wondered if I had accidently sat on one of the twigs we were using for the fire, but as I continued to listen I heard more snapping's somewhere in the forest. I couldn't exactly tell where the snapping was coming from because each time I heard it, it sounded like it was coming from a different spot. I became more and more terrified.

Eventually after a few minutes I got up and went over to Gwen and started shaking her awake. "Gwen. Gwen," I whispered frantically to her.

"I hate you, Dad, I did the right thing," I heard her mumble in her sleep. I was taken aback by this for a moment, wondering what she was dreaming about, but the snapping continued and I shook her harder, trying to get her to wake up.

"Gwen, Gwen," I said whispering urgently to her. "Dad. Dad?" she muttered as she slowly opened her eyes. After she was fully awake Gwen gave me an annoyed look. Obviously she didn't like me waking her up.

"Dad what are...?" She tried to say in a normal voice before I cut her off.

"Quiet," I whispered, "listen."

We sat there for a couple of minutes in complete silence. Eventually Gwen too heard the noise in the trees.

"What is that?" She asked getting up and walking slowly over to where she thought the snapping was coming from. I was growing incredibly nervous and I tried to usher Gwen to come back but she kept going. Pipsqueak had also been woken up, his feathers turned back into their normal red-and-gold flames. As Gwen approached the spot where she thought the snapping was coming from I began to hear another strange noise. It was almost like a deep, rumbling

89

sound, and like the snapping, I also heard it in different spots. As I sat there, fear growing inside me, wondering what was going on, there came a blood curdling scream as Gwen shouted, "in the trees! Now!"

Gwen threw herself out of the way as the beast who had been circling us launched itself at Gwen. Gwen darted up the side of a tree and onto one of the top branches. Pipsqueak screeched and took off, flying as high as he could. I meanwhile had done nothing but stand there in fear as the creature turned its attention toward me. It was huge! It had the head and body of a lion, with each paw containing three claws that were three inches long. A long scorpion tail with a six inch stinger at the end and giant bat-like wings added to its fearsome appearance. But most frightening of all were the three rows of razor sharp teeth it had in its mouth. It was a *manticore*!

The manticore roared as it tried to swipe me with one of its huge paws. I had gotten over my initial fear and managed to jump aside from the swipe. I then rolled underneath the beast when the manticore tried to pounce on me, causing it to smash its head into a tree.

"Come on Dad!" Gwen yelled. I got up and sprinted over to the tree that Gwen had climbed, but since I wasn't acrobatic like her climbing the tree was difficult. I was almost near the top branch that Gwen was on when I turned and saw the manticore recovering from its pounce. It whirled around and started charging towards me.

"Hurry Dad!" Gwen yelled, sticking her hand out for me to grab. I reached out trying to grab it but it was too late. The manticore jumped and took a swipe at me and one of the claws met its mark on the back of my right leg.

The pain that I felt was excruciating. All the pain I had experienced in my life was nothing compared to this. It felt like my entire body had been split open. I yelled in agony as I let go of the branch I was holding. As I fell Gwen reached out and grabbed me and very slowly started pulling me up. The manticore, who realized he hadn't

90

killed me yet, was looking to make another jump. I knew that if the manticore made another swipe, it would be the end of me.

Then just as the manticore looked like he was ready to pounce, a blur of red and gold flew past me and hit the manticore dead straight in the head. The manticore recoiled in pain and I saw that it was Pipsqueak. The manticore recovered and roared in anger at my tiny defender. The manticore tried to attack Pipsqueak any way it knew how. It pounced on him, swiped at him with his claws, it even tried to hit Pipsqueak with its scorpion tail, but every time Pipsqueak would dodge the attack and start attacking the manticore's face.

As I watched the fight my vision started to fade in and out. One moment I could see everything just fine then the next everything was a blur.

"Hang on Dad," Gwen shouted, even though I could barely hear her as it sounded like she was miles away.

Gwen managed to pull me up to the branch she was sitting on. She laid me against the trunk and I could tell by her face that I wasn't doing too well. My vision was completely blurry and I only saw rough outlines of objects. I could still hear Pipsqueak and the manticore fighting but their squawks and roars sounded distant to me. I was still in agonizing pain, but I also felt myself growing hotter, like I had been out in the heat for hours. Soon everything around me was going dark. I tried to look around but that only gave me a massive headache and made everything worse.

Somewhere out in the distance I heard Gwen shouting, "Dad! Dad!" very faintly. That was the last thing I heard before everything went black.

Chapter 9

Out of the Forest

I was dead. Or at least that's what I thought for a split second when I saw nothing but darkness. However I soon realized that I wasn't dead when I felt a cool breeze brush over me. I began opening my eyes, but a bright flash of light caused me to immediately shut them.

After a few moments I started opening them again, only more slowly this time. After my eyes had gotten fully adjusted to the light I realized that it was morning. The sun shone brightly over the trees, and there was a gentle breeze blowing through the forest.

The first thing that I saw when I opened my eyes was Gwen. And she looked terrible! Her eyes were bloodshot, her hair was messier than usual, and a piece of her nightgown was torn off. Just looking at her I could tell she had been up all night.

I groaned and stirred a little to let her know I was awake. Upon hearing me Gwen jumped and got into a defensive position. When she saw that I was the one who made the noise she let out a sigh of relief.

"Oh thank goodness, you're awake," she said getting up and walking across the tree branch. I tried to sit up but as I did I felt light-headed again and fell right back down.

"How long was I out?" I asked feebly.

"Surprisingly only a couple of hours," Gwen said, "I stayed up all night to make sure that the manticore didn't come back."

"What happened to that thing anyway?" I asked.

"Oh don't worry," Gwen said giving a devilish smile, "little brother over there took care of him." Gwen pointed to the end of the branch we were sitting on and I saw Pipsqueak sitting there watching us. As soon as Pipsqueak saw me looking at him the baby bird gave a happy squawk of delight before taking off. The small bird tried to fly close and start nuzzling me again, but thankfully Gwen shooed him away before he could set any of my clothes on fire.

"Pipsqueak managed to fight the manticore off. I didn't know the little guy had it in him," Gwen said giving Pipsqueak, who had given up on nuzzling me and went back to flying around our heads again, a small smile.

"Well, I'm glad to see you two are getting along now," I said noticing Gwen's smile, "I hate seeing my children fight."

"Oh shut up," Gwen said rolling her eyes and chuckling. I couldn't help but laugh too, but as I did I noticed something that almost made me throw up.

Wrapped around my right leg was the missing piece of Gwen's nightgown, completely covered in dried blood, however it wasn't the dry blood that almost made me sick; it was the area around the bandage which had turned a sickly earth-green color. Seeing my leg like that made me want to pass out again but I managed to stay calm as I slowly reached out and touched the place where the nightgown covered my cut. I instantly recoiled in pain.

"Don't touch it!" Gwen said slapping my head which was already hurting.

"Sorry," I said, "it's just that, it looks really bad."

"Well, be glad it's only a scratch," Gwen said.

"A scratch!" I said in amazement, "You call this a scratch!" Gwen slapped me again.

"Yes," she said, "I cleaned your wound. The cut didn't go too deep. If it did, you probably would've died. But thankfully I managed to make you a splint, you'll live."

"Oh," I said a little taken aback by Gwen's knowledge of treating wounds, "well, thanks."

Gwen nodded, "Don't mention it. Anyway we got to get moving, we need to get out of this forest before sunset. I don't want to spend another night in here with all those creatures lurking around," she said.

"Ok, but we have one problem," I said trying to sit up, "I can't move my leg."

"I know, I know!" Gwen said a little agitated. Gwen thought for a moment before she started undoing the bandages around my leg.

93

I turned away, not wanting to see what the actual wound looked like. I heard Gwen muttering to herself, trying to figure out what to do.

"Hold on I got an idea," she finally said. Gwen got back up and started climbing down the tree. "Wait here until I get back," she said.

"Oh yeah, I definitely thought about leaving," I said dryly.

"Ok let me rephrase that, keep *quiet* until I get back," Gwen said. I snickered a bit.

"Oh don't worry, you won't hear a thing out of me," I said as Gwen got to the bottom of the tree.

"Yes, I bet I won't," Gwen muttered as she walked off into the trees. I laughed.

I started getting worried. It had been a long time since Gwen wandered off into the forest and there was no sign that she would be returning soon. I sat on the branch, occasionally shooing Pipsqueak away, wondering why she had to go into the forest and what had happened to her. Most of the things that I thought about involved Gwen lying in the forest somewhere either mangled or torn to shreds. I tried to push those thoughts out of my head the best I could.

Another thought that occurred to me frightened me even more. A picture of Gwen walking through the forest, talking to herself about how glad she was to get rid of the deadweight. I shuddered at that thought.

"Don't worry, Gwen would never do anything like that, right?" I whispered, trying to calm myself down. An image of the bartender from The Forest Inn, his hands around Gwen's neck, strangling her and saying how this was payback for what we did to him was another torment. Knowing how absurd the idea really was though, this thought didn't stay in my head for very long.

Finally after waiting for a while I started to hear rustling leaves and snapping twigs. I looked down and saw Gwen reemerge from the forest with something in her hand.

"Oh good. I was starting to worry I'd have to come in and get your body," I said jokingly.

"Ha, ha, very funny," Gwen said as she started to climb the tree again.

"What took you so long?" I asked when she got up on our branch.

"Sorry, but it took me a while to find this," Gwen said sticking her hand out.

Inside her hand was some sort of flower. It was bright gold and had six points which sloped upward. "What is that?" I asked her.

"It's a Heamed flower," Gwen answered.

"A what flower?" I asked.

"He-med," Gwen pronounced. "The Royal Guard sometimes uses its nectar to heal injuries."

"Really? How come I've never heard about it before?" I asked, looking at the flower.

"It was first discovered on the original quest to find The Time Stone. The guard doesn't use it that much though. It grows deep in The Dark Forest so that makes it incredibly hard to find," Gwen explained as she started to undo the cloth wrapped around my leg.

"And you're sure this is going to help?" I asked.

"I think so." Gwen said.

"Oh that's comforting," I said dryly.

"Well it would be better if the nectar was made into some kind of medicine, but I'm pretty sure the nectar alone will help soothe some of the pain," Gwen said. She finished untying my bandages and I turned my head again while she started working on my leg. "Now this should only hurt a little," Gwen reassured.

A little turned out to be a lot. As soon as the nectar from the Heamed flower touched my wound, I was once again hit with a wave of unbearable, agonizing pain. I shut my eyes tighter and gritted my teeth as it felt like a sword had just gone through my leg. I let out a

95

low moan and hoped that it would be over soon. I thought I heard Gwen say something, but I was in so much pain that I couldn't even hear her. Seconds past and still the pain continued. It felt like my leg was on fire and no amount of water could put it out. Then just when I started wondering when this torture was going to end--it did.

The pain suddenly subsided, replaced by a feeling of relief. Every drop of nectar that was applied to my wound was now healing instead of hurting it. I opened my eyes and unclenched my jaw as I let all the pain in my body release. Any amount of discomfort I had seemed to be melting away with every drop. I turned my head back toward Gwen and for the first time got a good look at my wound. And I have to say, it wasn't that bad.

It wasn't anything worth celebrating over, but it definitely wasn't as bad as what I thought it was going to be. The way I had imagined my cut, was at about 2 inches deep, with massive amounts of dried blood and pockets of oozing puss all over it. However, the wound looked more like a large cut rather than a trauma wound. It was definitely deeper than most, but not as deep as what it felt like, and there was not as much blood as I expected.

Gwen looked up and saw me examining my wound. "Told you that nectar stuff works," She said grinning.

"Yeah, exactly," I said stupidly as I looked at my leg and wiggled it back and forth. My leg hurt, but since the nectar had taken most of the injury away, I knew I could walk. Gwen finished putting nectar on the cut and retied my bandages. "How long does this stuff last?" I asked her.

"I don't know," Gwen said getting up, "when it's done right, the effects can last about two weeks, but here..." she trailed off.

"Oh," I said glumly, now thinking about how my agonizing pain could possibly return at any time. I looked up at Gwen and saw she too looked depressed, like she was mad at herself for not being able to fully fix me.

"Well then," I said in a determined voice, trying to cheer Gwen up, "we better hope we make it to The Time Stone before that happens."

Gwen smiled at my eagerness. "Come on Dad, let's get going."

Let's get going was easier said than done. Although the Heamed flower's nectar had healed my leg, it was still incredibly stiff. It took about half-an-hour, three slips, and a ton of cursing just to get me out of the tree. When we finally did make it out Gwen and I started walking in the direction that would take us directly out of the forest and to the edge of The Wasteland. Right behind us Pipsqueak zoomed around chirping happily. Every once in a while he would fly a little too close and Gwen and I would duck to avoid getting singed.

While we walked Gwen would pick some berries off some bushes, sniff them for a second, then either throw them on the ground or hand them to me. I tasted them and thought they were one of the most delicious things I'd ever eaten. But then again it was the only real food I had eaten in a couple of days, so I was pretty sure anything I ran into (besides slosh) would probably taste extraordinary. As I snacked on the berries I began to notice something strange.

I turned around and noticed Gwen lagging behind a bit. I thought it was strange because Gwen would usually be miles ahead of me and I would have to run just to keep up. At first I thought that maybe she was just going slowly because of my injury, but as I looked closer I could tell she was in some kind of deep thought.

"You know," I said chuckling, "I think you should be worried when your old man is quicker than you."

"What?" Gwen said looking up.

"Wow, and you're losing your hearing too? That's not a good sign," I said, now laughing.

"Shut up," Gwen said as she ran up to me, "I was just thinking."

"About what?" I asked innocently. Gwen looked at the ground and took a moment before answering. "About how to apologize," she said. "Apologize? For what?" I asked, dropping the innocent act. "For that injury," she said.

I paused for a moment, a little surprised at what Gwen was saying. "Wait, why are you apologizing? You didn't cause this," I said pointing at my leg.

"Well when you really think about it, if I hadn't accidently broken The Time Stone, you wouldn't have gotten that cut. So I guess it's sort of my fault," Gwen said.

I thought over what Gwen had said. There was some truth to that. I looked over at Gwen and saw from the look on her face this thing was eating at her.

"Hey don't worry about it," I said trying to comfort her, "Accidents happen, you didn't mean to get sent back in time."

"Yeah, right," Gwen said, still staring at the ground.

"And besides," I continued, "Look at how many jams you've gotten us out of. I'm pretty sure I would've been chopped up and used for slosh if it hadn't been for you!" Gwen started to perk up a bit.

"Well, let's just say I had a good teacher," she said punching me in the arm a little too hard.

"Hey don't mention it," I said rubbing the spot she hit.

"What are you talking about? I meant Stewart." She said, giving me a confused look.

I laughed but my laugh soon turned into a small chuckle.

"Uh, you were kidding right?" I asked. Gwen gave me a sly smirk and I let out a sigh of relief. "Anyway," I said, getting back on topic, "After all the things I've seen you do, I don't think I could've picked a better second in command." Gwen's smile faltered a bit as she looked over at me.

"You mean that?" she asked.

"Yes, I do," I said confidently. Gwen took a moment to let what I told her sink in. She looked away and for a brief second I thought she had a small look of disappointment on her face. But when Gwen turned back towards me and gave me a warm smile I decided that I'd probably just imagined it.

"Thanks Dad," she said as she gave me a bone-crushing hug.

It hadn't been that long since our conversation when Gwen suddenly pointed, "There, I see it!" I jumped a good foot in the air.

"See what?" I asked.

"I think I see the edge of the forest!" Gwen said excitedly.

What! I said.

"Come on let's go!" Gwen said grabbing my arm and pulling me along behind her as she ran. I could tell Gwen was right. As we ran the trees started thinning out and when I looked up ahead I saw light filtering through high branches. Gwen and I broke into a sprint (which was incredibly difficult for me) and we finally burst through the other side of The Dark Forest.

The first thing that I did when we made it out of The Dark Forest was to fall flat on my face and start hugging the ground. "Oh fields, sweet, sweet, grassy fields," I said thankfully. I don't know how long I laid there in the grass. It could've been hours, but I didn't care; I was just glad to finally be out of that forest.

Suddenly I heard the sound of rushing water. I looked up and saw a sight that horrified me. Right in front of us was a large raging river, its water churned rapidly downstream, however that wasn't the terrifying part. On the other side of the river, stretching for endless miles, was a completely dry, rocky desert. Looking at the endless desert made me lose the good feeling I had gotten from resting in the grass. "Let me guess," I said, knowing but dreading the answer, "That's The Wasteland?"

"Yep," Gwen said who was scanning the desert like she was trying to locate something.

"Oh great," I said, "How are we going to find The Time Stone in there? That thing goes on for miles."

Gwen ignored my question as she continued to scan the rocky surface. After a minute of waiting, she spoke. "There," she said.

"What?" I said looking at her.

"Those two mountains in the distance," she said pointing, "That's where we need to go.

I followed where Gwen was pointing but I couldn't see any-thing. I squinted my eyes and looked and after about a minute I saw what she was pointing at. On the very edge of the horizon were, from what I could see, the very small and very faint outline of two mountains. In fact, they were so small and faint, if Gwen hadn't pointed them out to me, I would've completely missed them.

"Those are the mountains you told me about in your story," Gwen said, "That's where we need to go."

"So you expect us to walk across the entire desert?" I asked her in disbelief.

"Yes," Gwen simply replied.

"Well great," I said with a sigh.

Gwen looked at the sun which was sinking below the horizon. "We'll sleep here tonight. Tomorrow we'll try to find a safe way to cross that river, it's too dangerous to try and swim across. I'll keep watch tonight," Gwen said.

"Are you sure?" I asked her. Looking at Gwen I didn't know if she was well enough to keep watch. She still had bloodshot eyes and bags underneath them. "Yes, I'm sure, you have yourself a good night's rest," Gwen said shoving me to the ground.

"All right, all right, no need to get pushy," I said lying on the ground. I watched as Gwen went over to the edge of The Dark For-est and snapped a few twigs off one of the branches. She then came back over and arranged them in a pile. Pipsqueak swooped in and sat on one of the twigs, lighting it on fire. I smiled as I turned over. As I listened to the rushing water of the river I started feeling my eyelids getting heavy.

For the first time on this adventure I felt like I wasn't in any kind of danger. That allowed me to have time to think and as I felt myself drifting off I thought about my friends back home. King Cornelius, Queen Lana, Stewart, and especially Tamina. I wondered how they were reacting to me being gone. I wondered if they had sent anyone out to find me and what their reaction would be when I didn't turn up. The last thing I thought about before going straight to sleep was how I was going to explain all of this to them if I managed to survive this journey.

Chapter 10

A Nightmare Come True

That night's sleep was probably the best thing that I had in days (next to the nectar from the Heamed flower). Finally there was genuine peace and quiet. No angry bartender trying to kill us, no mythical creature trying to tear us to shreds, and no more being in The Dark Forest. Finally everything was going smoothly. Or so I thought.

As I slept I had a bizarre dream that involved me fighting a giant version of the manticore from The Dark Forest. The manticore was once again trying to tear me to bits, but unlike last time my leg was fully healed and I had a sword to defend myself with. The manticore kept swiping at me with its giant claws, trying to land a blow, and I had to keep ducking out of the way to avoid getting ripped to shreds.

As I continued to battle the giant monster, out of nowhere I suddenly heard Gwen's voice somewhere in the distance. "Dad!" I heard her yell. I groaned and turned over in my sleep, thinking that it was just part of the dream. I managed to dodge one of the manticore's attacks and slashed at it with my sword; cutting off its scorpion tail. The manticore roared in pain and I took the chance to jump on top of its back.

Just when I was about to deliver the finishing blow however, I heard Gwen's voice again. "Dad!" she yelled, only louder this time and in a more panicked tone. I stirred in my sleep again and tried my best to ignore Gwen's voice, however after the third time I heard her voice I realized that it wasn't part of my dream. I began to slowly open my eyes, a little annoyed that Gwen had woken me up. Fighting that giant manticore had strangely felt very satisfying, almost like I was getting my revenge on the real one for what it did to my leg.

As I woke up I could tell that it was still night out. *"Wonder what Gwen wants?"* I thought to myself as I let out a big yawn. Part of my brain was still asleep so I wasn't really thinking clearly at that moment. *"If Gwen's trying to wake me up that probably means..."* And then my brain suddenly turned on as I realized something very bad was probably happening. I sat bolt upright, fully awake, and saw something that I was completely unprepared for. Something that I knew would haunt my nightmares for the rest of my life.

On the ground, with her hands tied behind her back, struggling to get free, was Gwen. Next to her was Pipsqueak who was also tied up and screeching madly. Towering above them, with a hand on Gwen's shoulder, was the black outline of an incredibly tall man. Or at least I thought it was an outline of a man until I realized that the man *was* the outline.

Somehow, in a way that I could never truly describe, this guy seemed to be made out of nothing but darkness; almost like a human shadow had gotten up off the ground and became a living creature. The only thing that wasn't pitch black about him were his eyes, but that was only because he didn't have any. Instead he had two giant holes going straight through the front of his head.

After having a run in with a baby phoenix and almost being eaten by a manticore, seeing this, "shadowy" thing right in front of me shouldn't have been all that frightening, but the way the shadowman looked just made me freeze in terror.

"Why hello there," The shadowman said in a deep, raspy voice that made me shiver.

"Dad! Ru..." Gwen tried to yell before she was suddenly silenced as shadows materialized around her mouth.

"It's very rude to interrupt, my dear," The shadowman said to Gwen. Gwen glared at the figure, but he just ignored her and turned his attention back to me. "I happened to be passing by and I noticed your campfire. I hope I'm not intruding," he said. The shadowman waited for me to answer, but I was so terrified by the fact that he could talk even though he had no physical mouth that I found myself unable to speak. The shadowman continued to wait and I knew that I had to say something, and soon.

"Who...Who..." I started to say, but I was so stricken with fear that I wasn't able to finish. The shadowman however seemed to know what I was implying.

"Oh of course, where are my manners," he said. The shadowman took his hand off of Gwen's shoulder and I saw a look of relief wash over her face. He took a small bow almost like he was showing respect, but with the situation Gwen and I were in, it might as well have been an insult. "My name is Lord Tharon. Third Generation of the royal family. Son of High King Damien. Defeater of the Wicked Horned Dragon. Conqueror of the Veod tribe, and Ruler of Dovania," He said in an overly-dramatic voice. "And who might you be?" he asked looking up.

"Uh, I'm...Sam," I squeaked out. Tharon looked at me for a second and it felt like he was staring directly into my soul.

"Indeed," he finally said in an unenthusiastic voice. Apparently he was expecting me to say something more.

However Tharon didn't have long to dwell on the lack of achievements in my life because right then Gwen had decided to be...well Gwen. Gwen suddenly jumped to her feet, but Tharon seemed to know exactly what she was planning and pushed her back to the ground. "Well, well, looks like we have a feisty one here," he said as Gwen struggled to get free.

"So my dear, what's your name?" Tharon asked as he bent down to look at Gwen. The shadows that covered Gwen's mouth suddenly melted away and Gwen took a couple of deep breaths before answering.

"I'm someone who doesn't like being tied up," Gwen spat at Tharon sarcastically. I saw Tharon's eyes narrow. Obviously he didn't like Gwen's attitude. Tharon got right up next to her face and glared at her with both holes for eyes.

"I'm sorry my dear, but I don't think I've explained yet," he said dropping his voice to a low growl, "I don't have a sense of humor." I looked at Gwen and saw that although she had a stern look on her face, she too was terrified like me. I signaled to her, trying to silently tell her to tell him her name before he did something bad to her. Gwen looked over at me, saw what I was doing, then sighed.

"My name is Guinevere" she said looking back at Tharon, "Second-In-Command of King Stewart's Royal Guard."

"Really!" Tharon said in an impressed voice that was so obviously fake, "Second-In-Command? That's quite an accomplishment. More than I can say for your father."

After hearing that last sentence both Gwen and I looked at Tharon in shock. "What...How..." Gwen asked in disbelief.

"Oh I know a lot more than you think my dear," Tharon said interrupting her, "I know all about The Time Stone and your little quest to find it." Tharon then suddenly grabbed Gwen by the back of her nightdress and Pipsqueak who was still screeching wildly and dragged them both over and sat them down right next to me. Seeing Gwen being manhandled like that made me feel angry and looking at Gwen I could tell she felt the exact same way.

"How do you know about The Time Stone?" Gwen asked after Tharon had let her go.

Tharon gave a raspy, bone-chilling chuckle, "My dear, haven't you ever heard about the story of The Time Stone?" he said. Gwen seemed to be taken aback by that question. She was silent for a moment before answering.

"Yeah. A lot of people know about that story," Gwen said, giving Tharon a confused look. "A kingdom of sorcerers one day gave a stone the power to control time itself. But realizing the stone could be used for evil the sorcerers sealed it away."

After Gwen had finished her brief summary of the story Tharon looked at her. "What! That's it?" he asked, almost sounding surprised.

"Uh Yeah, that's it," Gwen said looking back at him confused.

"You don't remember anything else about the story!" Tharon said.

"That's it," Gwen said, confused by what Tharon meant, "That's the entire story."

If Tharon had eyes I was pretty sure he would have been rolling them. He let out a high pitched sigh that almost made my ears bleed. "Of course they would change that part of the story," Tharon said, talking more to himself than to us.

Both Gwen and I looked at each other in confusion. "What do you mean, *they* changed the story?" Gwen asked, looking back at Tharon.

Tharon looked over at us for a second, probably thinking about whether or not he should tell us anything, before answering. "There's more to that story my dear," he said.

"What do you mean there's more to the story," Gwen asked.

"There's a whole other part to the story of The Time Stone my dear," Tharon answered. "But it would seem those wretched sorcerers have erased it. I guess they thought it might have been too scary for small children," Tharon said in a sarcastic tone I didn't know he was capable of having.

"What are you talking about?" Gwen asked. "You see my dear," Tharon continued, "I too, am part of The Time Stone legend. In fact, without me, there wouldn't have even been a legend at all."

Gwen looked at Tharon like he was crazy. "That's impossible," Gwen said, "The Time Stone was created over a thousand years ago. How could you be a part of the story?" Tharon gave a small, menacing chuckle.

"Oh, I'll tell you my dear," he said, pausing for a while before he began speaking.

"You see, long ago, I was once the ruler of Dovania, a small but well-respected kingdom. For many years I watched over my people, wanting nothing more than to protect them from any kind of danger. Soon word reached me about an item that could make that want into a reality. A stone that allowed the holder to control time itself had been created by our neighboring kingdom, Morendale. Well, you could imagine my reaction when I heard about the stone's power. I was mystified but also ecstatic. Can you picture that kind of power? Any battle I ever lost, I could redo. Any mistake I ever made, I could go back and fix. I knew that this was my chance. My chance to keep Dovania safe and make it last forever. So I went to the King of Morendale and humbly asked for The Time Stone. However, I was rudely turned away."

"Really? They didn't give someone like you an all-powerful artifact that could control time itself? Gee, I wonder why?" Gwen sarcastically said under her breath. Everything got quite. Even Pipsqueak went silent. I looked at Gwen in horror. Tharon shot Gwen a nasty look, clearly angry that he had been interrupted. I held my breath, not knowing what was going to happen next, but knowing one thing. Gwen was almost certainly dead from that comment.

To my surprise however, Tharon began to laugh. A slow, menacing, evil laugh. "You think I was always like this?" he asked Gwen.

"Well, Uh..." Gwen started. Tharon didn't let Gwen finished though, and just continued talking.

"Believe it or not my dear I was once human as well. A tall, muscular, handsome human I might add. But that all changed on the day I asked for The Time Stone."

"How?" I asked, finding myself getting strangely engrossed in Tharon story.

"You see," Tharon said continuing, "After the king had refused to hand over The Time Stone, the sorcerers who created it put a curse on me that transformed me into *this*," he said pointing at his body. "After that they imprisoned me inside The Time Stone and locked me away forever."

I listened to Tharon finish his story. Even though I found his story interesting I could definitely tell that Tharon was lying. A lot of his story didn't seem to add up. Plus, I wouldn't expect someone like Tharon to be very honest. However, I wasn't going to start arguing the validity of his story with him right now, if ever.

"For over a thousand years I've been trapped inside that stone, and now I finally have the chance to take my revenge on that pathetic little kingdom," Tharon said, his back turned towards us.

"So what does wanting revenge have to do with us then?" Gwen asked.

"Because my dear," Tharon said turning around and facing her, "ever since I was released from The Time Stone, I've had a question on my mind. It's a question only you can answer. Why did you release me?"

There was dead silence once again. Nobody talked. Nobody moved. I wondered if anyone even breathed. After hearing what Tharon had said Gwen suddenly went all white, her eyes grew wide, and her breathing slowed; it was like she was in some sort of trance. I looked back and forth between Gwen and Tharon, wondering what Tharon was talking about.

"What do you mean, Why did she release you?" I asked. "Gwen never released you." Tharon looked at me and I could tell he was annoyed that I was talking to him.

"I was trapped in The Time Stone." he said. "She was the one who smashed it and broke the spell that was imprisoning me wasn't she?"

I looked down to avoid making direct eye contact with him, "Well, yes. But she didn't know you were in there. She smashed it accidently," I said trying to sound braver than I was actually feeling. Tharon just gave me a pathetic look and turned back towards Gwen.

"Come on my dear. Why don't you tell me what really happened."

"I told you how she broke it," I said, becoming a little agitated.

"Really?" Tharon said in a sarcastic tone, turning back toward me, "you expect me to believe that she smashed an ancient, all-powerful artifact by pure accident?"

"Accidents happ..." I started to say before I caught sight of Gwen.

Gwen had snapped out of her trance and her head was now pointed at the ground, looking at random objects. She had that look of depression from yesterday again.

"Gwen?" I asked concerned. Gwen looked up, locked eyes with me for a second, and then quickly turned her attention back towards the ground. Wherever this was going I didn't like it. "Gwen?" I asked again in a more worried voice.

"Come dear," Tharon said taking Gwen's chin and raising it up so that they both stared at each other, "I think it's time to tell your father the truth now."

"Tell me what?" I asked her.

"Nothing," Gwen said shooting me another look.

Tharon chuckled again. "My dear, please. I know when someone is hiding something, and you seem to be hiding something big. Now we are all friends here, why don't you come and share it with us?"

Gwen shot me another look and I could see she was indeed holding something back from me. "Gwen..." I started to say before Gwen cut in.

"I'm not second-in-command," she quickly said before looking back at the ground. It took me a moment to fully grasp what she said but when it did I just stared at her in confusion.

"What do you...?" I started to say before I saw Gwen taking a couple deep breaths and I knew she was going to continue so I stopped.

"It was my first mission." Gwen started. "It was supposed to be a simple one. A couple of thieves had kidnapped this kid and were holding him for ransom and we were called in to get him back. When we got there you told me to wait behind and keep watch while you tried to negotiate with them. But while you were gone I saw this opening and I thought I could get in there without anyone seeing me. I managed to sneak in and get the kid out safely, but when I was riding back with him one of the thieves must have spotted me. Soon we were all under attack and...and..." Gwen seemed to be having a hard time telling the next part of the story.

"You can be honest dear," Tharon said in a fake sympathetic voice, "how many died?" Gwen shot Tharon a dirty glare before continuing on.

"Anyway, when we got back you were furious with me. You told me that I wasn't ready to be in charge. You said you made a mistake by making me in Second-in-Command, so you took it away.

I was so mad at you! We got the kid back safely, that's all that mattered right? We completed the mission. It didn't matter *how* it was completed. I tried telling you that but you didn't even listen. Eventually I just gave up and ran off. I didn't know exactly where I was headed, but somehow I ended up in the room where they kept The Time Stone. Seeing it made me think about you and what you told me. I was so mad that I...well, you know. Before I knew what was going on there were all these flashing blue and white lights and then, nothing. The next thing I knew I was waking up in the middle of The Dark Forest."

I listened to Gwen finish her story. After she was done I did nothing but stare at her in complete and utter silence. I would've liked to describe what I was feeling right then but that would've been impossible, because at that point I was feeling *everything*. Confusion at what I'd just heard. Pity for what happened to Gwen. Happiness for the kid who got back safe. Frustration for having Gwen lie to me. But most of all I felt angry. Angry at Gwen for getting me into this situation. Here I was, out in the middle of nowhere, getting myself into dangerous situations, being dragged to a place that most likely I wouldn't even come back from, and now to top it all off, I was being held captive by a man made out of total darkness; And all because Gwen didn't follow instructions.

I was unable to think of anything to say, I hoped beyond anything that Gwen had made the whole story up as some kind of cruel sick joke, however as I looked at her the look in her eyes told me that she wasn't making any of this up. I couldn't take it, I literally felt like my head was going to explode. On the other hand, Tharon seemed to be more delighted than ever as he seemed to have a twinkle in his holes for eyes.

"Well, well, isn't that most depressing," he said in an upbeat attitude. "However, I must thank you my dear. You've given me all the answers I needed." Gwen said nothing and only looked at the ground. "As thanks for your cooperation, Tharon said, "I'd like to leave you with this gift."

110

Tharon waved his hand and the shadows that were holding Gwen and Pipsqueak disappeared into thin air. Pipsqueak screeched and immediately took off in fright. Tharon then snapped his fingers and, in an image I'll never get out of my head, somehow actually made the night morph and twist itself into the shape of a wolf. The shadow wolf sprang to life and growled as it moved towards us, baring its incredibly long, black teeth.

"The journey ends here for you two," Tharon said laughing as the wolf advanced on us.

I almost froze at the sight of the wolf. It may have been only made out of shadows, but my guess was it was still going to be super painful when it tried to eat us. The wolf continued to slowly advance, its back arched. I looked around trying to find something, anything, that could get us out of this situation, but it was hopeless. The wolf was in front of us, the raging river was right behind us. There was no escape route. We were cornered. I closed my eyes and turned my head and waited for the wolf to start sinking its fangs into me.

However certain death never came. Instead there was a loud thud and a yelp. I opened my eyes and saw that Gwen had kicked the wolf in the mouth when it tried to attack, knocking it backwards.

"Come on, run!" Gwen yelled as she jumped to her feet.

"Where are we supposed to go?" I asked her.

Gwen never answered my question. Instead she quickly grabbed the back of my shirt, yanked me to my feet, and started dragging me along behind her. Gwen then did something that I thought was the craziest (or perhaps more accurately the stupidest) thing that she had ever done. Gwen, still holding on to me, dived headfirst into the raging river behind us.

Chapter 11

A Terrifying Discovery

It was the crack of dawn, the sun was barely over the horizon, and already Tamina was up, more energized than ever. Stewart on the other hand was a different story. After he and Tamina had followed the footprints all the way to The Dark Forest's main path, Stewart suggested that they should stop for the night. Tamina was hesitant at first, wanting to keep going, but after some persuasion Stewart managed to convince her.

Stewart said that he'd keep watch for the night; partly to keep Tamina safe, but mostly to make sure that she didn't try and sneak off. So while Tamina went to bed Stewart gathered supplies to get a fire started. When morning finally came Tamina awoke to find that Stewart hadn't gotten any sleep which meant he was very irritated.

After repacking everything and putting their fire out Tamina and Stewart set off again, mostly riding in silence. Tamina didn't want to say something that would set Stewart off. After riding for a couple of hours Stewart happened to spot something that made him stop. "Tamina, look!" he said. Tamina stopped and saw what Stewart was looking at. Nailed to the side of a tree was a wooden sign that said, *The Forest Inn*.

"Come on, let's check this place out. Maybe we can sleep here tonight." Stewart said happily.

"I don't know," Tamina said hesitantly, looking down the main path, "we should probably just keep going."

"You know, it's possible that Sam was here and someone knows where he is," Stewart said trying to convince Tamina. After hearing Sam's name Tamina immediately perked up and thought for a moment.

"Well, I guess we can check it out," she said.

Stewart smiled, trying to remain professional while on the inside there was an entire celebration going on. "Right this way your

Highness," Stewart said eagerly, gesturing down the side path that led to the inn. Tamina giggled at Stewart's over-eagerness and Stewart blushed when he realized what he was doing. Stewart and Tamina rode down the side path and when they reached the clearing they both gasped in horror.

The inn was in shambles. Windows were broken, debris was scattered all over the place, and much of it looked like it had burnt down. If they hadn't seen someone moving around inside Tamina and Stewart would've thought that The Forest Inn was abandoned.

"Something tells me we're not going to get good service here. Or any kind of service for that matter," Tamina said, giving Stewart a worried look.

Tamina and Stewart got off their horses and cautiously walked up to the front door. Stewart noticed that the door was hanging open like someone had forcefully opened it. He paused for a second and looked at Tamina who only shrugged before stepping inside. "Hello," he called out.

Suddenly a big gruff man appeared behind the front counter brandishing a knife at them. Stewart immediately drew his sword.

"Who are you?" the man yelled, sounding terrified.

"My name is Stewart, head of King Cornelius's Royal Guard, and this is Princess Tamina. I suggest you put that knife down right now," Stewart said, pointing his sword at the man. Upon hearing Stewart's statement the man behind the counter lowered his knife and looked between Stewart and Tamina.

"Wait, you two aren't working for that creepy shadow guy are you?" he asked.

Tamina and Stewart looked at each other in confusion.

"Uh No?" Tamina answered, having no idea what the man was talking about. The man looked at them for a moment before letting out a huge sigh.

"Um, sorry about that," he said, setting the knife down and coming out behind the counter, "I guess I've just been a little on edge ever since that weird shadow guy came in here yesterday looking for those two kids." Stewart looked at the man in confusion. He had no idea what the man was talking about but he knew one thing; *this man was clearly crazy*. However, even though he thought the man was completely insane, Stewart did find something the man said very interesting.

"Wait a minute. What do you mean...?" Stewart started to say before he was suddenly pushed out of the way by Tamina.

"What kids? Who are you talking about? Do you know where they went?" she yelled in excitement as she grabbed the man's shirt and started shaking him viciously.

The man froze in fear, "Uh, wha...Um..." he stuttered, terrified at Tamina's outburst.

"Tamina, calm down!" Stewart said jumping up and prying her off the guy. After being released the man took several steps back, fearing for his life, afraid of what Tamina was going to do to him.

"Sorry about that," Stewart said as Tamina took several deep breaths to calm herself. "What she means is, we're looking for someone. A boy. About thirteen. Have you seen him?" The man didn't speak at first, afraid that if he said anything else Tamina would lash out again, however, he did finally answer.

"You're looking for those kids too?" He asked.

"You've seen Sam?" Tamina, half excited and half crazy. The man took another step back from Tamina.

"If you're talking about that one scrawny kid, yeah, I saw him," the man said cautiously, "He came in here with some girl a couple of days ago. They tried ordering some food without paying. After that they destroyed my Inn then took off." The man gritted his teeth and balled his fist at that last part. "Then just yesterday this weird, "shadowman" thing shows up and asks whether or not I've seen them." Tamina and Stewart listened to what the man said intensely. After he had finished Stewart thought about what he had just heard.

At any other time Stewart wouldn't have believed the man's story. But looking around the destroyed inn something inside Stewart told him that the man was actually telling the truth. But if the man was telling the truth, then that only left Stewart with more questions than answers. *Sam came in here with a girl? Why did Sam destroy an entire Inn? What was he talking about, a shadowman?*

All these questions made Stewart's head hurt and only added to the complicated mystery finding Sam was turning out to be. After thinking for a moment Stewart pushed all questions he had out of his mind, deciding to focus on finding Sam first and then solving this bizarre mystery later.

"Did he by any chance mention where he was headed?" Stewart asked.

"Said they were headed to The Wasteland," the man answered.

Upon saying the word Wasteland all life in Tamina and Stewart seemed to be sucked out as both of them became cold and stiff. Tamina looked at the man in shock, unable to believe what she'd just heard.

"Wh...Where, did you say he was headed?" she quietly asked, hoping that she had misheard him, panic building inside her.

"The Wasteland," the man said, staring confusingly at Stewart and Tamina who both were staring at him with blank faces.

After hearing the man confirm where Sam was headed, Stewart slowly turned around and locked eyes with Tamina. Tamina and Stewart just stood there staring at each other, both unable to find the will to speak or to fully grasp what they had just heard. Then after a long time of just staring at each other, without any warning, Tamina bolted straight out the door.

"Tamina wait!" Stewart yelled as he ran after her.

Tamina wasted no time. She quickly jumped on her horse and started riding off. But before she could go very far Stewart ran right in front of her. "Tamina stop! I know what you're doing and you're going to get yourself killed," he said.

"We've got to stop Sam before he gets to The Wasteland," Tamina said, desperation in her voice.

"Tamina listen, something weird is going on. That bartender said that Sam was traveling with some girl, and he said that some creepy, "shadowman guy," was looking for him. Something's not right," Stewart said.

"That's why we need to find him before he gets hurt," Tamina said, becoming more agitated at Stewart's seemingly uncaring attitude towards finding Sam. Tamina started riding off again but Stewart stopped her again.

"Tamina I'm saying this because I care about you," Stewart said, "I can't let you do this."

"What? And you don't care about Sam?" Tamina yelled, snapping at Stewart. Stewart jumped back in shock. Even though he had known Tamina for years now, never had he heard her yell like this before. It seemed to be a mixture of anger, sadness, panic, and worry all at the same time. As Stewart looked at Tamina trying to think of something to say, he happened to notice something that he hadn't seen before. Tamina seemed to be holding back tears.

"Uh...I..." Stewart said trying to say something. Tamina only rolled her eyes as she cracked her horse's reins and rode off into The Dark Forest towards The Wasteland. "Tamina, Tamina wait!" Stewart yelled as he too jumped on his horse and rode after her.

As the two rode off into The Dark Forest the man from the inn watched them disappear from the broken door. "What was that about?" he asked.

"Tamina, Tamina wait!" Stewart yelled as he rode after her. Tamina ignored him as she continued to ride deeper into The Dark Forest. Stewart gritted his teeth and he spurred his horse, desperately trying to catch up to her. After chasing after Tamina for a while Stewart finally managed to ride up along beside her.

"Tamina stop!" Stewart yelled at her. Tamina only shot him an evil glare before continuing on. "Tamina please," Stewart yelled, nearly pleading at this point. Stewart didn't know whether Tamina was going to stop or not, but to his surprise Tamina suddenly pulled back on her horses reins, making it come to a quick halt. Stewart slowed down and jumped off his horse and ran over to Tamina who glared down at him.

"What?" She said harshly.

116

Stewart stood there trying to think of something to say to her, but all he could come up with was, "Tamina look, I'm sorry ok."

"Sorry? That's all you can think of. I'm sorry?" Tamina said in disbelief, getting off her horse too.

"Tamina look," Stewart said, trying to find the right words to say, "I care about Sam too, ok. But I can't...I can't just let you run off and get yourself killed."

"Really?" Tamina said not buying what Stewart was saying, "This entire time all you've wanted to do was give up and go back home, and yet you actually say you *care* about Sam?"

"Tamina..." Stewart tried to say, but it looked like Tamina wasn't done talking.

"I mean, it doesn't bother you that Sam could be in some kind of horrible danger?"

"Tamina..." Stewart tried to interject again, seeing Tamina getting more and more worked up.

"It doesn't bother you that he could be sick? It doesn't bother you that he could be lying somewhere hurt? It doesn't bother you that he could be... that he could be..." Tamina couldn't finish her last sentence. With each word she said her breathing became shorter and shorter and soon she began to feel weak.

Tamina leaned against a tree and took several deep breaths, trying to calm herself down and as she did she felt tears forming in her eyes. She sniffed and wiped them away, hoping that Stewart wouldn't see her crying. After her eyes were dry Tamina looked up and saw Stewart watching her, a concerned look on his face. Tamina stood back up, took one final deep breath before walking back over to her horse and climbing on.

As she rode past him, Tamina stopped in front of Stewart and said, "Sam's out there somewhere, and I'm going to find him, no matter what."

"Tamina," Stewart said, finally able to say something, "I do care about Sam, but my first priority is keeping you safe. I'm just trying to look out for you. It's my job to protect you and your family." Stewart waited for Tamina to respond.

"Sam is family…," was the only thing she said.

"Wait, what?" Stewart said, surprised by the answer Tamina gave him. Tamina turned away from Stewart and looked at the forest ahead of her. She started riding off, but before she did she said one final thing to Stewart. "…at least, that's what I always thought."

Stewart watched as Tamina rode off, still shocked at her reply. Stewart got back on his horse and started following her. As he followed her Stewart thought about Tamina's last words and the way she had acted, and as he did it became clear to him why Tamina was so determined to find Sam. Ahead of Stewart, Tamina rode in silence, tears still in her eyes. As she rode she silently prayed that they would find Sam soon.

"Don't worry Sam," she quietly said, trying to reassure herself more than anything else, "Everything's going to be ok."

Chapter 12

Battling a Rock Slide

Everything was not ok. As soon as Gwen and I hit the water the river's current forced us both apart and I went spinning off downstream, tossing around like an out of control ragdoll, smashing into the river's sides. I desperately flailed my arms around, hoping I would manage to grab hold of something, anything, that would stop me from being carried away. Every once in a while I would surface but a huge wave would hit me and force me back down before I could get the chance to take a breath. I was quickly running out of air.

As I continued being thrown around downstream I suddenly felt my body hit against something hard. Without really considering what it was I quickly reached out and grabbed it, hoping that it would stop me. However, as I turned to look at what I had grabbed I saw through the muddy river water the very faint outline of a person. I had managed to grab hold of Gwen.

Gwen, from what I could tell, was trying hard to fight against the river's current too. Her body twitched and jerked as she tried to swim upstream and it made it incredibly difficult for me to hold onto her. Every once in a while her body would move in a way that would almost make me lose my grip and I had to grab on tighter so that I wouldn't accidently let go of her and be swept away again. Gwen and I continued being carried downriver, Gwen desperately trying to fight against the current and me desperately trying not to lose hold of her.

Then, just when I started to feel like I was about to pass out again, a miracle happened. All of a sudden I felt myself slowing down. I opened my eyes and saw that while Gwen and I were still being carried downriver, the current wasn't as quick or as forceful. Before I had the chance to react I suddenly felt myself being pulled upwards. I turned my head and saw Gwen pulling on my arms as she lifted both me and herself up towards the top of the water.

As soon as we broke through the surface Gwen let go of me, and waves upon waves started slapping me in the face, filling my lungs with water.

"Come on move!" I heard Gwen shout. Gwen took off swimming towards the opposite side of the river. I was completely exhausted, yet despite that I turned in the direction Gwen was headed, mustered up all the strength that I could, and started swimming after her.

Swimming after Gwen was painful. Both my arms and legs were numb and every time I moved one of them it felt incredibly uncomfortable. Eventually though I managed to make it to the other side of the river. Gwen was already on shore waiting for me with her arm outstretched. I grabbed her hand and together with our combined strength, or at least Gwen's strength and whatever I had left, we managed to get me pulled ashore.

As soon as I was on dry land I collapsed to the ground. I laid there on the shore completely drenched, frozen to the bone, desperately gasping for air. After several minutes (or it could've been several hours I couldn't really tell) of nothing but heavy breathing and trying to calm myself down, my breathing steadied. I started to pick myself up but as I did, I winced as I felt a small pain in my leg. I looked down at my bandaged leg and moved it a bit.

Once again I felt a small pain shoot through it. I silently cursed to myself. Either the river had washed some of the nectar away or the nectar's effect were just fading. Either way, the pain in my leg wasn't a good sign. As I looked up from my bandaged leg I finally realized just exactly where Gwen and I were.

We were on the other side of the river. I stood there staring at the very edge of The Dark Forest on the other side. I looked down at the ground and saw that I was standing on dried dirt and rock. I turned around and looked behind me and saw miles and miles of endless open desert. We had finally made it. Gwen and I were in The Wasteland.

"We...We made it," Gwen said as she sat there doubled over, panting heavily. I continued looking out over the endless, barren desert, and as I did Gwen's story came flooding back to me.

"Yeah," I said glumly, a depressing feeling growing inside me, "It's great we got away from that shadowman thing." I heard Gwen stand up behind me and pause for a second before she spoke.

"Dad look, I know you're mad but..." Gwen started to say before I cut her off.

"Mad? No, I'm not mad," I said calmly turning around to look at her. I could tell by Gwen's skeptical expression that she didn't believe me. I could tell that she was expecting me to do something like start screaming at the top of my lungs, but believe it or not, I actually *was* telling the truth. I wasn't mad, at least not anymore. At first I was. At first I was furious. But all that fury seemed to have been washed away when we had plunged into the river. Now I was experiencing something very different, something worse. Stupidity.

I was now mentally hitting myself in the head over the entire situation I was now in. Here I was, on a life-threatening adventure, an injured leg, practically starving to death, heading towards a place no one has ever came back from, and to top it all off, we were now being hunted by an all-powerful demonic being; and all of it because of my own daughter from the future. There were no amount of words that could be used to describe how stupid I felt for getting myself roped into this. The feeling was truly awful. I locked eyes with Gwen and with one look at each other both of us could tell how the other person was feeling.

Gwen could see just how stupid I felt, having left my entire life behind to go on a life-threatening journey, and I could see how depressed and miserable she was for having caused this whole predicament. We stood there for a while just staring at each other, not saying a word, both lost in our own thoughts. At one point Pipsqueak came flying down and landed beside me, but he seemed to know something was wrong because he just sat there silently, not even attempting to try and nuzzle me. Finally after who knows how long of nothing but looking at each other I realized that just standing there was getting us nowhere.

"Come on, let's go," I said sullenly as I turned around and started walking off.

I hadn't even gone three steps before Gwen said, "Fine. If you don't want to help me anymore then I guess I'll just go by myself," in a somewhat irritated tone. Hearing Gwen speak to me like that made me feel annoyed.

I stopped dead and turned around to face her and firmly said, "You know what? No. You asked me for my help so that's what I'm going to do. Now come on!"

Gwen stood there, completely stunned by my blunt response. Gwen looked at the ground and shifted her feet a bit, unable to come up with a retort. "I didn't want it like this," she whispered glumly. Looking at Gwen part of my annoyance disappeared as I felt a small bit of pity for her. I turned around and started walking away but as I did Gwen seemed to be determined to have the final word.

"You know, I asked for your help and you said no. But you still came after me. Why?"

Now it was my turned to be completely stunned. I stopped dead in my tracks again and turned back around and saw Gwen looking at me, waiting for me to answer. *Why did I follow Gwen?* I thought. I specifically told her I couldn't, and Gwen seemed to be fine with that answer, but at the last possible second I had decided to go after her.

Why though? I stood there for several minutes racking my brain trying to come up with an answer. *"Why was I here?"* The question kept spinning around my head, yet no matter how hard I tried I couldn't come up with a reason for why I had followed Gwen. Finally after several minutes of trying to come up with an answer I just gave up.

"I don't know." I said sighing heavily, "I just… I don't know."

I looked at Gwen and saw that the look on her face was worse than depressed. I could definitely tell that my answer wasn't the one that she wanted to hear. Gwen sighed and walked up to me and for

122

a split second I thought she was going to hit me, but instead she did something that was probably worse. She just walked right past me.

"Come on, let's go," she said depressingly. I watched Gwen walk away, her head hanging low and her shoulders slumped. Seeing her like that made me feel even worse than I already did. I opened my mouth to say something that would make her feel better but I immediately closed it, not wanting to make things worse. Instead I just started following her, but I made sure to keep my distance. Behind me Pipsqueak unfolded his wings and took off flying overhead as together all three of us made our way into The Wasteland.

For two days Gwen and I walked without saying a single word to each other. We just continued to trudge through the dry, rocky desert, both of us trying to ignore the blazing heat as we made our way towards the mountains. While we were walking my stomach began to rumble and that was bad since there was literally no food or water for miles. My leg had also gone back to hurting again. It wasn't really pain, more like extreme discomfort, but it was obvious the effects of the Heamed nectar were gone, so I had to limp along behind Gwen which slowed us both down considerably. Gwen and I never stopped to sleep. We didn't even stop to rest. We just kept on walking and by the end of the second day it felt like I was ready to collapse again. But still I pressed on, my mind too preoccupied with other things than about how my legs felt as if they were about to fall right off.

It did occur to me, *what would happen to me* if *we actually made it to The Time Stone.* If Gwen and I somehow both survived this journey and we managed to get Gwen back to her own time, what would happen to me? I would be stuck out in the middle of The Wasteland all by myself. Sure I'd have Pipsqueak and he would do a pretty good job at defending me, but I doubted I'd ever manage to make it back home. I thought about bringing this up with Gwen, but with the current state of things I thought it would be best just to keep my mouth shut.

So for many more hours Gwen walked and I did my best to keep up as I hobbled along behind her with my bad leg. Pipsqueak flew above us and never once did he try to fly down and nuzzle me. Maybe the baby phoenix could tell just how grave the situation was, or maybe our depression was contagious. Either way, the complete lack of any personal interaction was driving me crazy. After a few more hours of nothing but walking in silence I was sure that I was about to go insane when suddenly...

"Hey Look!" Gwen said. I jumped back in shock, it was the first time that either one of us had spoken since we first started walking. Even Pipsqueak squawked in surprise.

"Gah! She speaks!" I said, trying to seize the opportunity to lighten the mood. Gwen shot me a look of both confusion and annoyance and I quickly said, "Um, sorry, you were saying?" Gwen dismissed what I'd said and turned back to what she was looking at.

"Look," she said, pointing to something in the distance. I followed where Gwen was pointing and saw that a few hundred feet away from us the ground seemed to just drop off like it was the edge of a cliff.

"What is that?" I asked. "I think I know, come on," Gwen said. Gwen then took off running which surprised me since I half expected her to start telling me what the cliff was exactly. I started running after her, a sharp pain going through my leg with every step I took. After a few minutes Gwen stopped and I managed to catch up with her. After stopping I started massaging my leg, trying to soothe the pain. When the pain had subsided I looked up and saw that the thing Gwen had been pointing at wasn't a cliff, but a canyon.

The canyon itself wasn't very deep, nor was it very wide. But what it lacked in width and depth it certainly made up for in length. The canyon stretched on for miles both east and west. Looking at it I knew that there was no way Gwen and I were walking along the edge of the thing until it ended, that left us with only one other option. "Yep this is it," Gwen said.

124

"What is?" I asked. "The canyon from your story. You told me that you had to cross this to get to The Time Stone," Gwen said looking over the side, "Looks like we'll have to make our way down to get across." I nodded and as I stood there looking down into the canyon my legs started to feel like they were about to give way; we had been walking for so long that I was now on the verge of collapsing.

"Ok, here's what we do," I said, "I say we rest here for the night and then when morning comes we..." I stopped as I looked back up. Gwen had mysteriously vanished. I looked around to see where she was but she was nowhere to be seen. "Gwen!" I called out.

"Come on Dad!" I heard her shout. I turned around and looked back down in the canyon and saw that Gwen was already climbing her way down. I silently groaned and gritted my teeth as my entire body ached from tiredness. However, ignoring my yearning for sleep and against my better judgment, I made my way over to the edge, got down on all fours, and slowly started climbing my way down after Gwen.

Climbing down was an incredibly rough thing to do. First off, my leg was still aching, so constantly moving it around was not a pleasant experience. Secondly, almost every time I moved the rock beneath me would shift which resulted in me almost losing my footing. And lastly, I was so tired that I constantly felt like I was going to accidently let go of the side and fall. I looked over at Gwen to see how she was doing and I saw that she was having practically no trouble at all.

In fact, watching her was almost like watching her swing from the tree branches in the forest. Gwen would be clinging to the side of the canyon then she would look below her as she tried to find the next place she could grab hold of. After finding the next spot that she could cling to, Gwen would quickly let go of the side, plummet a few feet, then reach out and grab the side of the canyon again. I sat there amazed at Gwen's skill. I continued to watch her until she finally reached the bottom of the canyon.

"Come on, hurry up!" Gwen yelled, looking up at me. I suddenly snapped back to reality as I realized that in watching Gwen I had completely forgotten that I was still holding onto the canyon wall.

I slowly started making my way down towards the bottom of the canyon again, however, this time it was even more difficult. With all the time that I had spent watching Gwen my hands had become all sweaty which meant trying to hold onto the canyon wall was a challenge. I made my way down towards the ground again, trying hard to ignore the pain in my leg. Every once in a while I would lose my grip, but thankfully I managed to cling to the rock wall. Eventually after many grueling minutes I finally felt my feet touch ground.

"Made it!" I said happily.

"Finally," Gwen said, starting to laugh. I looked at Gwen, a little shocked to see her laughing again.

"Oh shut up," I said laughing a little too, glad to see Gwen in a happy mood again.

After Gwen and I finished laughing I started looking around the bottom of the canyon and I noticed something very strange. All along the ground were dozens (if not hundreds) of rock piles, and when I mean rock piles I just don't mean rocks and boulders thrown all over the place. These rock piles were all stacked and neatly organized into big individual piles. With any other situation I would've dismissed the strange way the rock piles looked, but after Pipsqueak, the manticore, and the encounter with Tharon, the look of the rock piles just felt unnatural. I didn't like it.

"Are you..?" I asked Gwen.

"Yeah," she said, knowing what I was going to ask her. Gwen had the same worried look as me as she too eyed the rock piles suspiciously. "Come on, let's get out of here before something bad happens," She said.

I nodded and Gwen and I started making our way across the canyon, both of us walking faster than normal and keeping more alert. Gwen and I were about halfway across the canyon before Pip-squeak decided to swoop down and sit on top of one of the rock piles. That's when everything went downhill.

At once the pile let out a loud rumble that sounded like a creature growling. Pipsqueak squawked in fright and took off in the air. Gwen and I stopped dead in our tracks and looked at the rock pile. The pile shifted as the rocks and boulders all started to move around as the loud rumble continued. Panic struck both Gwen and I as we both shot each other terrified looks.

"Run!" We both yelled in unison.

Gwen and I took off as fast as we could. As we ran past more rock piles it was apparent that whatever Pipsqueak had done it had started a chain reaction. Every pile we ran past was now shifting and making the same rumbling sound. Gwen and I started to run faster as the rumbling sound continued to grow louder and louder.

When Gwen and I reached the other side of the canyon Gwen held out her arms. "Come on, I'll help you up," she said. I placed my leg in her hands and Gwen hoisted me up. I started climbing along the side of the canyon, not daring to turn around to see what was happening behind us. My leg still hurt while I climbed, but I was able to ignore that since it was the least of my problems.

As I inched upward I suddenly heard Gwen shout, "faster, hurry!" in an urgent tone. I turned and looked down to see that Gwen was right below me, climbing right after me. As I started to turn my attention back to climbing, I accidently caught a glimpse of what was going on behind us and was frozen there on the canyon wall in complete terror.

The piles of rocks had formed together to create numerous rock monsters. Each monster was about nine feet tall and was made out of an assortment of rocks. Giant boulders made up their bodies, feet, and heads while smaller rocks seem to comprise their arms and hands. I could also see that large, jagged stones made up the monsters teeth and claws. I stood there in complete and utter shock. It was like the time I first caught sight of the manticore, only this time I knew it was going to be about a hundred times worse.

These rock monsters were way bigger than the manticore, looked way more powerful, and there was more than one--more like one hundred.

One of the rock monsters (I'd assume he was the leader because he was bigger than the others) let out a deep, low roar. When the one rock monster roared it caused the ground to shake a little. However, when all the other rock monsters started to roar too that caused an entire earthquake. I desperately clung to the side of the canyon hoping that I wouldn't let go.

"Come on, move!" I heard Gwen shout. Gwen's shouting snapped me out of my daze and I began climbing the side of the canyon again, faster than ever this time. As I climbed, I turned back around to see what the rock monsters were doing and it just so happened that they were now focusing all of their attention on us.

The leader of the monsters roared one more time and started charging at us. I panicked as I saw the beast barreling towards us and started to climb faster, praying that another miracle would happen. And it just so happened a miracle did occur. Pipsqueak once again came to the rescue as he came blazing out of the sky and shot directly at the rock monsters. Pipsqueak hit the lead monster square in the head and while it didn't stop him, it did manage to confuse the creature. It also caused the poor phoenix to go limp and fall to the ground after hitting solid rock. The rock monster roared as it tried to stop and see what had hit him. Unfortunately, the creature wasn't able to stop in time and it ran right against the canyon wall. The entire canyon shook violently. So much so that it was too much for Gwen and I to hold onto and both of us went plummeting towards the ground.

When I hit the canyon floor the first thing that I heard was the massive, CRACK, that was obviously my back. I yelled in pain as it felt like it was completely broken. I tried looking around but my vision had gone all blurry again, so it was hard to make anything out. I did manage to see the rock monster stumbling back and made out the other monsters looking confused as to what had just happened.

I heard a loud groan off to my left and I turned to see what it was. To my horror I saw that it was Gwen lying there motionless.

"Gwen!" I yelled feebly.

I tried to get up, but the pain in my back caused me to fall back to the ground in agony. I looked at the rock monster and saw that it was dazed from hitting the side of the wall and the other monsters were all looking at it, unable to figure out what they should do without its direction. I turned back towards Gwen and slowly started to crawl to her. As I made my way there, the pain in my back increased and my vision became blurrier. I knew it was only a matter of time before I would pass out again.

I managed to make it to Gwen and when I did I saw that she must've hit her head pretty hard because she was completely knocked out. I turned around to see that the rock monster had gotten over its confusion and now had his attention back on us. It was obvious that he must've thought that Gwen and I were the ones who attacked him because it roared in anger and the other rock monsters followed his example.

I knew the leader was going to try and charge us again, but this time it would be worse. The other monsters around him looked like they were going to charge at us too. I looked over the entire situation. Both Gwen and Pipsqueak were passed out, I was about to pass out too, my leg and probably my back were broken and a whole horde of rock monsters were about to squish us. I looked down at Gwen feeling hopeless, but when I saw Gwen's unconscious face I knew that I had to do something.

Using all of my remaining strength, I managed to crawl on top of Gwen and shield her. I knew that it was useless, but it was the only thing I could think of doing. As soon as I was on top of Gwen I felt myself slipping out of consciousness. Before I did, I sat there and watched as all the rock monsters started charging us again. I knew that this was the end for Gwen and me.

Then just when I was about to pass out, I thought I heard people. People shouting. And not just a small group of people, but it sounded like a whole army of people, all yelling in unison. I watched in disbelief as suddenly strange blasts of energy came zooming out of nowhere and hit the rock monsters. All the rock monsters roared in pain and stopped. Some of them were reduced to rubble while others started retreating, all of them trying to get away from the mysterious energy blasts.

I couldn't believe what I saw. At first I thought that it was just the blurry-black vision from me passing out that was causing it. However, right before I passed out again I heard footsteps behind me and then I heard someone faintly shout, "I found them." After that I did finally black out.

Chapter 13

My "Daughter" Tells All

"Are you sure I added enough?" I heard somebody say faintly. I stirred a little as I slowly opened my eyes. After my eyes had fully adjusted to the light I looked around and realized that I was now lying in an incredibly soft, and incredibly comfortable bed. I tried turning my head to see where I was but I couldn't make anything out because my vision was still blurry. From what I could see though, it looked like I was in some sort of large room with dozens of beds all lined up next to each other. Looking at it, I guessed that I was in some sort of infirmary.

There were windows all along the right wall and the light shining in from them told me that it was morning outside. On the right side of my bed was a small wooden table with a birdcage on top of it. Inside that birdcage I could make out Pipsqueak, fast asleep. I turned to my left and saw that the bed right next to mine was also occupied. I couldn't see the person lying in it, but looking at the blurry image I could instantly tell that the person was Gwen.

I lay there watching Gwen, wondering whether she was going to be ok or not, and as I did, I once again heard people talking. I turned and looked down towards the foot of my bed and saw the blurry outlines of two people. For a split second I almost couldn't believe it. Even though I couldn't exactly see them any clearer than what I assumed to be Gwen, both outlines had a striking resemblance to Cornelius and Tamina. *Could it be?* I thought. *Am I really home?*

The two people seemed to be talking to each other about how to make something, however, I was so dazed that everything they said made no sense to me at all. From what I could tell the girl seemed to be standing over a cart with a pot on top of it. The man sitting down at the edge of my bed seemed to be giving her instructions.

131

I let out a small groan as I tried to sit up, however as I did my back started to ache. My groan seemed to have woken Pipsqueak up because the birdcage began to rattle as the small phoenix started to chirp happily. The two people at the end of my bed turned silent as they saw me trying to push myself up.

"Careful," the girl said rushing over and pushing me back down onto the bed, "don't try to move, the medicine hasn't taken full effect yet."

"Sorry Tamina," I said as I laid back down. I saw the girl look over at the man sitting at the end of the bed before looking back at me.

"Tamina? Who's Tamina? My name's Rachael," she said in confusion. After hearing the girl say her name I took one of my hands and started hitting the side of my head lightly until my vision came back into focus. When my sight had fully restored itself I saw that it actually *wasn't* Tamina.

This girl was much younger than Tamina; she looked like she was about Gwen and my age. She had dark brown hair, light blue eyes, and an eloquent sounding voice.

"Sorry," I said, blushing a little as I realized my mistake, "I thought you were someone else."

Just then a low moan filled the entire room. Both Rachael and I looked over at Gwen's bed and saw that Gwen had started to wake up. Rachael ran over to her and pushed her back down.

"That goes for you too," she said. Rachael moved in front of Gwen so I couldn't see what was going on, but I suddenly heard Gwen making weird gasping noises like she was choking.

"Take it easy," Rachael said as she tried to calm Gwen down, "Don't get yourself all worked up." After Gwen had stopped making the weird choking sounds Rachael walked back towards her cart and I saw that Gwen had a look of absolute horror. She started darting her eyes around the entire room and I could tell by her face that Gwen did not want to be here. Her eyes finally landed on the mysterious man sitting at the end of my bed and I heard Gwen's breathing cut short. "Great," she whispered through gritted teeth, "Morendale."

I had no idea what Gwen was talking about, but just then Rachael came back again with two small cups in her hand. "Here drink this. This should help you both feel better," she said handing the cups to us. I took the cup from Rachael but Gwen was a little bit slower at reaching for it. From the look she was giving it, it looked as though she thought the cup was poison. After getting my cup I tried taking a drink from it, but since I was still laying down most of the liquid just spilled onto my bed.

"Oh here, let me help you," Rachael said as she came over and helped me get into a sitting position. After helping me up Rachael moved over and started helping Gwen too.

"Thanks," Gwen said quietly to her. I started to drink the liquid Rachael gave to me, but as soon as the liquid touched my mouth I felt like I was about to throw up. I gagged as I tried my best to hold back the vomit that was forming in the back of my throat.

"I know, it's horrible," Rachael said chuckling.

"What? No, it's not horrible," I said sarcastically, "I just think it would taste better if it was more like slosh. What is this stuff anyway?"

Rachael gave a little smile, "Sorry," she said, "its medicine made from Heamed flower nectar. It is great at healing, but it doesn't make a very compelling drink, does it?" I shook my head as I continued to sip my drink, holding my breath and doing my best to ignore the nasty taste. As I drank I happened to look over at the end of my bed and I noticed that the mysterious man was still watching us.

The man had somehow managed to look both young and old at the same time. I would say that he looked to be about in his thirties, however there were wrinkles all over his face, and his hair and beard were completely gray. In his hand he held a giant walking stick and looking at it I wondered if it had ever been used to hit people with. He had the same color of eyes as Rachael, however, they did

133

not look as kind as hers. Looking at him I knew that this was a man I shouldn't cross.

As I sat there and drank my medicine the man continued to just sit there and watch Gwen and me. I tried ignoring him while I drank, however my eyes always kept focusing back on him and seeing him sitting there made me incredibly uncomfortable. I looked over at Gwen and saw that she had her eyes buried in her cup, she too looked uncomfortable. In fact, she looked even more uncomfortable than me. Every once in a while Gwen would look up from her drink to stare at the man, then when she saw that he was still looking at us she would quickly glance back down at her cup again.

Gwen and I continued to sip our medicine, doing our best to hold it down and to avoid making eye contact with the mysterious man. After all of the drink was gone Gwen and I handed both our cups back to Rachael.

"It shouldn't be long before you start feeling better," Rachael told us.

"Rachael can you please excuse us," The mysterious man at the end of the bed said, speaking for the first time.

The room became completely silent as we all turned towards him. "Yes, of course Father," Rachael said. Rachael brought the cups over and sat them down on the cart and started walking towards the door. As she left I stared at her and thought, *wait father?* After Rachael had exited the room and closed the door the room became dead silent again. Nobody talked, moved, or even breathed. We just all sat there staring uncomfortably at each other, wondering what was going to happen next. Finally after a long moment of awkward silence the mysterious man spoke again.

"Very well," he said in a surprisingly patient voice, "I guess I'll start the introductions." The man got up and walked over to us, "I am King Leo, Leader of the Kingdom of Morendale. The girl who was just here was my daughter, Princess Rachael. And who might you be?" he asked us.

"Um, I'm Sam and this is Gwen," I said, stuttering a little. Leo came over and stuck his hand out.

134

"A pleasure to meet you," he said. I took his hand and shook it. Leo had a very firm grip, but not as firm as Gwen's.

"So um, where exactly are we?" I asked him.

"Oh of course, you're probably wondering," Leo said. "You three are in Morendale. My men and I managed to rescue you from those rock giants in the canyon."

"Rock giants?" I asked in confusion.

"Yes," Leo said nodding his head, "Rock Giants. Monsters that can only form at night. During the day they turn into lifeless piles of stone. We managed to rescue you and brought you past the mountains here to Morendale so you could be healed. Oh, but don't worry though, you've only been out for about two days," Leo quickly said noticing our stunned expressions.

I almost couldn't believe what I was hearing. Not only were Gwen and I rescued from rock giants by actual people, but those same people had managed to take us past the mountains we were already headed to. That meant that Gwen and I were closer than ever to The Time Stone.

And speaking of The Time Stone...

"And now that we have all of our history out of the way," Leo said, "I must ask you something." "And what's that?" I asked him. "Oh I'm not asking *you* anything my boy." Leo said turning around to face Gwen. "So my dear," he said looking directly at Gwen, causing her to quickly look away again, "Would you care to explain to me what happened to The Time Stone?"

Silence filled the room once again. I looked at King Leo completely shocked. "How, how do you know about The Time Stone?" I asked. Leo turned around and to my surprise, I saw a look of disbelief on *his* face. "What? You haven't figured it out yet?" he asked me. "Figured what out?" I asked, not understanding what Leo was getting at. "Remember what The Time Stone Legend said," was all Leo's response was.

I sat there and thought hard about the legend of The Time Stone, trying to understand what Leo was trying to tell me and after a couple of seconds of thinking I understood. "We're in…" I began before Gwen finished.

"We're in the kingdom of sorcerers," she said before adding quietly, "I was kind of hoping we would be able to avoid this place."

I stared at Leo in absolute disbelief. "You're a sorcerer," I said in amazement. Leo didn't say a word. Instead he just stuck his hand out and immediately flames erupted out of his palm. Pipsqueak squawked in surprise and I watched in complete amazement, my mouth hanging open as Leo made the fire dance around in his hand. "Does that answer your question," he said, seeming satisfied with my reaction. I nodded still unable to believe what I was seeing.

"And now my dear," Leo said extinguishing the fire and turning back to Gwen, "If you would be so kind as to explain to me what exactly happened." Gwen stared at the ground as she started mumbling incoherently.

"Wait, how did you know that the stone was destroyed?" I asked him. Leo turned back around and thought for a second before he answered. "I am a descendant from the original creators of The Time Stone." He started. "This means I have a special connection to The Time Stone itself. No matter where or when The Time Stone is, I will always be able to sense its power. And a few days ago I sensed that The Time Stone had been destroyed and that Lord Tharon had been released."

"Oh," Gwen quietly said surprised, "I didn't know you could do that."

"Yes, I can," Leo said turning back to her and smiling, "And I can also tell when a person is not in their right time period." Gwen's cheeks turned bright red as she looked down in embarrassment. Looking at Gwen I couldn't help but feel sorry for her. I thought about saying something to comfort her, but to my surprise it was Leo who said something first. "It's all right dear," he said in a soothing voice, "I just want to know what happened. I promise I will not yell or get mad at you. You have my word." I looked at Leo and saw the sincerity in his eyes and I knew he meant every word he said. Gwen finally looked up at Leo and when she saw that Leo wasn't

136

going to get angry at her she took a couple of deep breaths and started talking.

For the next twenty minutes Leo and I sat there and listened as Gwen told Leo about all of the events that led us to the canyon. She told him about her first mission, about how I had taken away her second-in-command position and how she had broken The Time Stone out of anger and ended up in the past. She went on to explain The Forest Inn, the manticore, Tharon, and finally the Rock Giants. While Gwen was telling the story, Leo never once interrupted. He just sat there in his chair and listened intensely to her. When Gwen reached the part about our run in with Tharon I could've sworn I saw Leo grip his walking stick more tightly and his jaw clench up a bit. Gwen ended her story with getting knocked off the canyon wall and passing out. "...And, I guess that's how we ended up here," she finished.

Leo sat for a while, thinking over what Gwen had told him. Gwen and I sat there and watched him, both of us holding our breaths, even Pipsqueak look anxious waiting for Leo to say something. Finally after waiting long enough Leo got back up and walked over to the sides of our beds. I waited for what he was going to say, but to my complete surprise the first thing he said was a question. A question directed at me.

"So you're her father then?" Leo asked me. I was taken aback by his question. With all the things Gwen described to him, him asking me whether I was her father was the last thing I had expected.

"Uh, yes, that's what Gwen told you," I said, confused.

"Mmm, how strange," Leo said looking between me and Gwen, "I really can't see any resemblance between you two, I expect you take more after your mother's side then?" he said addressing Gwen.

"Well um, actually no," Gwen said as I saw her become incredibly nervous, "You see...he's not actually my dad."

Silence filled the room once again. "Wait, What?" I asked in confusion.

"You're not actually my dad," Gwen repeated.

I stared at Gwen, completely dumfounded, unable to compre-hend what I was hearing. What did she mean, I wasn't her father. "What...But...I...You said..." I found myself stuttering.

"Oh no, you are my dad," Gwen quickly said starting to panic a little, "It's just that...Well I guess I should've told you before...But I just thought that it wasn't that important...But I guess you should know...it's just..." she stuttered incoherently.

I didn't hear what Gwen was trying to say. Instead I was too busy breathing heavily as I broke into a full-out panic at what I was hearing. *Gwen lied to me?* I thought. This whole time I had been on a life-threatening journey with someone who wasn't actually my daughter. So this whole journey had been a lie. I literally felt like I was going to pass out again as the room suddenly grew ten times hotter and everything began to spin. However, before I could do an-ything there was a loud thud as Leo slammed his walking stick on the ground. The room went silent again.

I immediately stopped my heavy breathing as Gwen and I looked at him. "Perhaps," he said looking at Gwen, "You would like to start over." "Yes," Gwen said quickly.

"Be my guest," Leo said smiling. Gwen nodded and took a cou-ple of deep breaths. I held my own breath as I waited to hear what she was going to say. "You see Dad," Gwen said looking at me, "What I'm trying to say is, I'm adopted."

I stared at Gwen, completely speechless. She continued before I could even speak. "You see my real parents abandoned me when I was a baby; they didn't even bother giving me a name." I saw Gwen clench her fist when she said that last part. "I grew up living on the streets. I stole food just so I could have something to eat." Both Leo and I listened to Gwen intently as each word she said only made us want to hear more.

"When I was about six Stewart and Tamina came riding through town. When they came by me I saw Tamina's crown and I thought that if I could get it that I could use it to get all the money I needed for the rest of my life. Well, I managed to snatch the crown when nobody was paying attention, but as soon as I did a bunch of

Royal Guards spotted me and started chasing after me. I tried to outrun them. I would've too, but a cat got in my way; the stupid hairball made me trip. I just remember lying there, hearing a bunch of horses circling me, and me just being so scared. I remember thinking that this was the end. Then I heard someone shout for everyone to stop."

"I looked up and saw you standing there. You told all the guards to back down, and then you asked me who I was. When I couldn't tell you my name you picked me up and put me on your horse, rode me back up to the castle, and gave me some food to eat. You showed me your room and said that I could sleep in your bed that night if I wanted to. After that you tucked me in and then you asked me… you asked me…" Gwen cut off at that last sentence and I was shocked at what I saw. Gwen was actually crying a little. She sniffed back her tears before continuing, "You asked me if I was willing to let you be my Dad."

After Gwen said that last sentence she looked up at me smiling and I looked back at her, again completely speechless. "Anyway," She continued, "I just couldn't believe it. Me with an actual family. No more living on the streets stealing food. I shook my head yes and after that you named me Gwen. So ever since that day I've been your daughter."

Gwen finished telling her story. After she was done I realized that tears had started forming in my eyes. I looked over at Leo and saw that there were small tears in his eyes too. Gwen waited for me to respond. I thought over Gwen's story and as I did I felt all kinds of emotion building inside me. "And why didn't you tell me this earlier?" I finally said smiling at her.

"What?" Gwen asked looking up at me in confusion.

"You do realize that I almost had a heart attack just now," I said sarcastically.

"Well, um," Gwen said, "I didn't want to tell you because I was afraid of how you would react. I thought that maybe you wouldn't help me anymore when you found out I wasn't *really* your daughter," she mumbled. I stared at Gwen with both a feeling of happiness and confusion.

"That is the stupidest thing you have ever said," I said, starting to laugh a little, "and that's saying something."

"What?" Gwen said looking at me.

"Why would you think that I wouldn't help you just because we're not related?"

"Um, I don't know," Gwen said looking embarrassed, "I guess it was just that I let my fears get the better of me."

After hearing her say that I couldn't help but smile, "Family's family, no matter if you're related or not," I told her. Gwen looked at me, and after seeing me smiling at her she smiled too.

"Well then," Leo said clearing his throat, "I'm terribly sorry for breaking up this wonderful moment, I really am, but I must leave to plan a course of action. With Lord Tharon on the loose we must act fast."

"Oh right, sorry," I said.

"Not to worry," Leo said holding up his hand, "The medicine should have taken effect by now. However I still want you three to stay here in Morendale tonight and rest. Also I would very much like for you both to join me for supper tonight. I will come and get you at sundown. Until then, good day." And with that Leo strode across the room to the door and exited. I looked over at Gwen and was about to say something but the door opened again and Rachael entered.

"If you please follow me," she said, "I will show you both to your rooms.

I pushed myself up and pulled the covers off my bed. That's when I saw that my leg had also been fully healed; no longer was it bandaged with Gwen's torn bloodied nightdress. Now I was able to fully move it without it hurting. Gwen got up out of bed too as Rachael went around to the right side of my bed and picked up Pipsqueaks cage. Pipsqueak cooed as Rachael pulled out some bird food for him.

140

"You have a lovely bird here," she said, "I don't think I've ever seen another animal that's as sweet as this one."

"Yeah well, he knows Mom will punish him if he misbehaves," I said sarcastically. Rachael laughed as she walked away. As we followed her I turned to see Gwen smiling. Gwen turned and saw me watching her. She gave me a warm smile and I couldn't help but give her one back too.

Chapter 14

A Day in Morendale

Tamina and Stewart rode through The Dark Forest in silence. After the incident at the inn the two had kept mostly to themselves. Tamina was still determined to make it to The Wasteland before Sam got there, and Stewart was still primarily concerned with keeping her safe. Eventually night fell and after they argued, Stewart managed to get Tamina to stop and sleep instead of pushing on in the dark. Stewart kept watch that night again and as he did, he noticed Tamina wasn't actually asleep, but was just lying there awake staring off into the forest. When morning came both of them repacked their things and took off again. Tamina suddenly spoke after riding in silence again for a few more hours.

"Look," Tamina said, sounding almost exhausted. Tamina pointed a shaking hand in front of her and Stewart saw that she was pointing to an area in the forest where the trees were thinning. "I think we're almost at the edge of The Dark Forest," Tamina said. She then galloped off towards the opening.

"Tamina wait up!" Stewart called, riding after her.

After a few minutes Tamina and Stewart trotted out of The Dark Forest and onto a patch of grassy field. "We made it," Stewart said happily as he closed his eyes and sighed with relief. Tamina didn't hear him. Instead she was busy looking around the field, looking for any signs of Sam.

"Where's Sam?" she said, worry in her voice. Stewart opened his eyes and looked around the grassy field and saw that he and Tamina were alone.

"We, we probably beat him here. Don't worry he'll show up," Stewart said trying to sound upbeat to comfort Tamina.

"Yeah, right," Tamina said, not sounding positive at all. Tamina lowered head as she started to ride off. "I think I'm going to ride a little," she said glumly, "You know, while we wait." Tamina rode off along the river. As Stewart watched her go he couldn't help but feel a little guilty. They had finally made it to the edge of The Dark Forest but Sam was nowhere in sight. A thought crossed Stewart's mind about where Sam was and... *No,* Stewart thought. Sam had to show up, he just had to. Tamina would kill him if he didn't. *That is if he already isn't...*Stewart shuddered as he pushed the disturbing image out of his head. *No, Sam is going to show up and everything is going to be fine.*

Right at that very moment he suddenly heard Tamina yell urgently, "Stewart come look at this!"

Stewart turned his horse around and rode quickly to where Tamina was. When he got there he saw why she had called him over. On the ground next to the river were the remains of a campfire. Stewart slid off his horse and started examining the fire. He couldn't tell how long the fire had been there but next to the fire he saw some imprints in the grass. The imprints were faint but there was no mistaking that they were made by a human. Looking at everything Stewart's blood became cold. He looked back at Tamina and he saw the look of worry in her face and together they both knew; Sam was gone.

Tamina felt her eyes begin to tear up. She couldn't believe it. She and Stewart had come all this way for nothing. Stewart got back up and tried to comfort Tamina, but he was unable to think of anything to say.

"Come on," he finally said glumly after a couple of minutes, "Let's head back." Tamina wanted to argue, but she knew that it was no use anymore. She just dried her eyes and nodded her head solemnly.

Stewart got back on his horse and turned around and started heading back towards The Dark Forest. Tamina slowly followed him at a distance, feeling completely defeated. Tamina turned back around and looked at the other side the river at The Wasteland. The endless desert stretched as far as the eye could see. Tamina stopped her horse and just stared off into the distance, and as she did, Tamina found her attitude beginning to change. No longer was she feeling defeated. Now she was feeling more determined than ever before. "Tamina come on," Stewart said, turning around and seeing Tamina looking at The Wasteland. Tamina looked back at Stewart and in a split second she made her decision.

Wheeling her horse around, Tamina rode straight over to the river and plunged into its depths. "Tamina!" Stewart yelled in horror. Stewart whirled around and rode straight up the river's edge. The river's waves were huge, but Stewart was able to see Tamina and her horse through them. Tamina was doing her best to try and cross the river but the river's current was too strong for her horse to handle and he was slowly getting pulled downriver. Without really thinking Stewart reined his horse into the water too.

The waves slapped him and his horse, threatening to carry them both downstream. Stewart did his best to keep his horse upright as he slowly pushed his way through the river towards Tamina. When Stewart was about a foot away from her, he reached out and grabbed her horse's reins and started pulling her horse after him as he tried to make it to the other side of the river. After many tense minutes Stewart finally managed to pull both his and Tamina's horse out of the water.

After they were safely back on shore both Tamina and Stewart slid off their horses and collapsed to the ground. Both of them sat there breathing heavily, both trying their best to calm down. After several minutes of deep breathing Stewart turned to Tamina and said. "He's your son, isn't he?"

"What?" Tamina said between breaths.

"Sam. You think of him as your son. That's why you went after him.

"Oh," Tamina said and Stewart could see her face growing a little red. "Well yeah. I mean, I've always thought he was, but I don't think he's ever felt the same way though." Stewart slowly nodded and smiled, finally understanding why Tamina was so determined. After all these years she regarded Sam as family. Stewart turned and

144

looked out over The Wasteland. Sam was somewhere out there. How they were going to find him, he didn't know, but they *were* going to find him.

"Come on, let's rest here for right now," Stewart said. He thought Tamina was going to object, but he was pleasantly surprised when she nodded in agreement. They started unpacking camp and no more than 10 seconds after they had done that did both of them passed out from exhaustion.

"Excuse me," a voice suddenly said. Both Tamina and Stewart stirred in their sleep as they started waking up. When Tamina and Stewart finally opened their eyes, they saw something they thought they never would see. Here out in the middle of The Wasteland was a group of, as far as Tamina could tell, thirty or so soldiers all riding horses. Upon seeing the soldiers, Stewart immediately jumped up and drew his sword in defense.

"Put the sword away, we mean you no harm," The leader said not even phased by Stewart, "We were just wondering who you are?"

"I am Stewart, Head of King Cornelius's Royal Guard and this is Princess Tamina, daughter of King Cornelius," Stewart said, "Who are you and your people?"

The leader of the group got off his horse and came over to them and bowed to Tamina. "your Majesty," he said, "We are from the kingdom of Morendale, and we have been sent to see if there are any other people out here."

"The kingdom of Morendale?" Stewart said confused. He had never heard of Morendale before.

"Wait what do you mean others?" Tamina asked.

"We found two people, a young boy and girl in the canyon a few miles from here. My Lord, King Leo, has sent us to see if there are any more people who may be out here in The Wasteland," The leader said.

Tamina felt her heart stop. "A boy!" she said almost shouting.

"Yes," the leader said not even shocked by her outburst, "Do you know him?"

"Yes," Tamina said excitement building in her, "Can you take us to him?"

The leader bowed and got back on his horse, "Please, follow us." Tamina couldn't believe it. They had done it, they were going to find Sam.

Tamina eagerly jumped back on her horse but Stewart stopped her and said, "Wait, I want answers. First off, who are you people?"

The leader only chuckled and said, "Come with us, I shall explain while we ride."

After she had led Gwen and I to the rooms we would be staying in, Rachael offered to show us around Morendale. Gwen declined Rachael's offer, however, I was excited to have a tour around the kingdom so I eagerly accepted. For the next couple of hours Rachael took me all around while telling me all about Morendale and its history. To some people, hearing about a place's history would be boring, but when you're in an entire kingdom where everybody's an all-powerful sorcerer, nothing about them is boring.

Rachael started by taking me through the castle and then making our way down to Morendale's village. All throughout the tour my mouth hung open as I was left pretty much speechless. Having grown up in a castle I was always impressed by the architecture and beauty of Cornelius' palace, but Leo's castle was another thing entirely.

This place was magnificent. That was the only way to truly describe it. Anyone who would've walked through the castle would've been awestruck like me. The castle was sculpted out of white marble, and its celling looked to be about 15 feet high. There were gleaming suits of armor and many bizarre-looking paintings and tapestries. Laid out over all the stone floors was dark purple carpet with a golden pattern sewed into it. Looking at it I wouldn't have been surprised if it was made with actual gold.

Rachael and I made our way down to Morendale's village. It wasn't as grand or as magnificent as the castle, however, compared

146

to my village back home, the architecture of the buildings was still very impressive. Rachael and I continued to walk until we came to a gigantic 30-foot stone wall that completely surrounded Morendale.

"And this is the wall that helps protect Morendale," Rachael said. She led me over to some stone stairs and we started climbing to the top of the wall. When we reached the top I saw guards positioned all along the edge. I ran over to the edge and looked out to see what was on the outside of Morendale. To my left I saw the mountains that led back to The Wasteland, to the right I saw another lone mountain in the distance and between that I saw miles of empty grassy fields.

"So what's this wall supposed to protect you from?" I asked, wondering why a kingdom of all-powerful sorcerers out in the middle of nowhere would need to worry about being attacked.

"My father said that the wall was built back when Tharon first declared war on us. Back when he first tried to seize The Time Stone," Rachael said coming up next to me.

"Tharon mentioned that he asked you for The Time Stone, he never mentioned a war," I said, remembering Gwen and I's encounter with the evil shadowman.

"Did you think he was telling you the truth when he spoke to you?" Rachael said turning and giving me a smug look.

"No, I gathered that much," I said smiling. Rachael chuckled. "So what really happened to The Time Stone? I mean, why are you guys so cut off from the rest of the world?" I asked Rachael.

Rachael's smile disappeared as her face turned a little mournful and sour. "Over there," Rachael said pointing in the distance. I looked at where she was pointing and saw far out in the distance something that looked like large piles of stone. "Dovania," Rachael said. "Tharon's kingdom," I finished, remembering the name from Tharon's story. Rachael nodded, "What's left of it anyway. My father told me that when The Time Stone had first been created Tharon came to Morendale and asked if he could have it. But the original king knew that Tharon would only use it to gain power, so he refused. Tharon was so outraged that he waged war on Morendale and attempted to take the stone by force. The creators of the stone were forced to strip Tharon of his soul and place it in The Time Stone."

"Why couldn't they just kill him?" I asked.

"We can't use magic to kill human beings," Rachael replied, "It's forbidden."

"Yeah, I'm pretty sure a guy made out of shadows can't really be considered a human being," I said jokingly. Rachael smiled.

"He wasn't always like that," she said, "People say that when Tharon was stripped from his body, his soul was so dark and twisted that it combined with darkness itself and he became that...*thing*."

Rachael finished and I just stood there thinking over what she had said, *"Ever since that day Morendale's stayed hidden. Keeping the stone safe."*

"Where is the stone?" I asked.

"There," Rachael said pointing to the lone mountain in the distance, "It's hidden at the very top." I stood looking at the mountain. We were so close it was almost like it being in reaching distance.

Rachael saw me looking at the mountain and said, "I don't think my father would like it if you'd gone running off and missed dinner tonight," laughingly.

"Oh, sorry," I said blushing a little. "Don't worry," Rachael said turning around and heading downstairs, "You'll get there soon enough."

"Yeah," I said following her, "I can't believe this whole thing's almost over."

As Rachael and I walked back to my room, she started asking me questions about my life. At first I was taken aback since life in Morendale was far more exciting than my life. But then I remembered that I was perhaps the first outsider she had ever met, so she probably found me as interesting as I found her. So I began telling her about my life, doing my best to make it sound as exciting as possible.

"So Princess Tamina, she's your mother?" Rachael asked after I told her about Tamina.

"What? Oh no," I said, "She's not my mom."

"But you told me she was the one who raised you?" Rachael replied.

"Yeah well, we're not related," I said.

"But aren't you the one who said family's family whether your related to them or not?" Rachael asked. After hearing Rachael say that I stopped dead. I stood there for a while staring off into space, my mind suddenly going into a deep thought.

"Yeah. Yeah I did," I said as something finally hit me.

"Hey, are you coming?" Rachael asked.

"What? Oh yeah," I said as I realized that I had just been standing there. I ran to catch back up to Rachael. We continued walking and I continued telling her about myself, but as we made our way back up towards the castle my mind kept wandering back to Rachael's comment. And from that moment on I knew that there was something that I had to do when this whole journey was over.

By the time we reached my room I had just finished getting through the whole adventure that led me here to Morendale.

"Well Gwen seems like a wonderful daughter," Rachael said.

"Yeah well, she can be a handful sometimes. She doesn't get if from my side that's for sure," I replied. Rachael laughed before she started walking out the door.

"My father will come and get you for dinner soon. Your clothes are on your bed," She said. I looked over and sure enough lying on top of my bed were newly folded dress clothes. "One more thing," Rachael said stopping in the door and turning around, "You told me you originally said no to Gwen. Why did you go after her then?"

My mind went completely blank. It was the same question that Gwen asked me right after the river incident and like when Gwen had asked, I still had no answer and I knew that *I don't know* wasn't going to work on Rachael. I racked my brain and finally after several minutes I said, "I guess, when I saw her asking for my help, I knew that she didn't really need it, but I could tell she wanted it. I could

149

tell she wanted me. I thought there had to be a reason, right?" I looked at Rachael wondering how she was going to reply and I was surprised to see her nodding her head in satisfaction and smiling.

"You're a great father," she said before she closed the door. I looked at the closed door stunned, but as I did, I could feel a small smile growing on my face.

Gwen lay on her bed completely bored. She had skipped out on the tour of Morendale, but that was only because she already knew her way around. That, and because of another thing that she didn't really want to think about. So for the next few hours Gwen did nothing but look up and stare at the ceiling.

Gwen's mind began to wander about several different things. She thought about how she had ended up in the past and about how she was going to have to apologize to everyone when she got back. She thought about Tharon, about being here in Morendale, about her dad, Rachael, Leo, and most importantly, she focused on getting The Time Stone and getting back home. With each of these things that crossed her mind, Gwen would take the pillow from her bed and hit it against her head. All of these thoughts made her head hurt. The one, however, that hurt the most was what was going to happen to her when she got home. "I'm so grounded when I get home," Gwen whispered to herself.

Just then there was a knock at Gwen's door and Rachael walked in. Rachael was wearing an elegant green ball gown and had her hair done up. In her hands Rachael carried a light-pink-colored dress.

"Hello," Rachael said walking over to Gwen's bed.

"Hi," Gwen said getting up.

There was a brief awkward pause before Rachael spoke again, "I, uh, managed to find you something to wear to dinner tonight," she said holding out the pink dress.

The dress wasn't as elegant as Rachael's, but it was still very fancy and Gwen thought it looked incredibly uncomfortable to wear. "Um, thanks, but I think I'll be ok," Gwen said.

"It's only for tonight, and besides, I don't think my father will appreciate you wearing that," Rachael said pointing to Gwen's tattered peach nightdress. Gwen wanted to argue, but she thought better of it so she just sighed and motioned for Rachael to hand her the dress.

"I'll be waiting outside for you when you're done changing," Rachael said.

She began walking away, but before she made it to the door Gwen said, "Actually, I need to ask you something." Rachael turned around and saw that Gwen's face had gone all red and she had her eyes pointed at the ground.

"Yes?" Rachael asked.

Gwen hesitated before answering. "Could you help me get ready?" she muttered, obviously embarrassed.

Rachael was taken aback by Gwen's request, but after seeing her embarrassed expression, she replied, "Oh, of...of course."

Gwen breathed a sigh of relief as Rachael went over and closed the room's curtains and got the pink dress. After Gwen had slipped the dress on Rachael started going around and making sure the dress fit ok.

"Um, thank you," Gwen said nervously, "it's just that I don't wear dresses a lot, so my mom always has to help me get ready for parties and things." Rachael stopped working on Gwen and looked at her in astonishment.

"You have a mother?" she said.

"Uh, yes," Gwen said, "Dad said he met her on one of the very first missions he went on." Just then Gwen let out a little yelp as Rachael tightened Gwen's dress a little bit too much. The dress may have fit Gwen, but it still made her feel like her ribcage was about to crack.

"Sorry," Rachael apologized, "Anyway, does your father know that you have a mother?"

"No," Gwen said, "I thought it would be better if he didn't find out, you know?" Rachael nodded her head in agreement and went back to tightening Gwen's dress.

"So," Rachael asked, "what's your mother like?" Gwen suddenly became nervous as the color drained from her face.

"Of course if you don't want to..." Rachael quickly said noticing the change in Gwen.

"No, no, I don't mind," Gwen said taking a few breaths. "She's smart, beautiful, caring, she always knows how to cheer me up," Gwen said, "She's also supportive, at least I think that she is."

"You think?" Rachael said in confusion.

"Well let's just say that whenever I go outside to practice with my sword I have to listen to a twenty-minute talk about how I need to be extremely careful, so I don't end up with only one eye."

Rachael chuckled, "Sounds like she's just looking out for you," she said.

"Yeah well, I just wish she didn't have to show it every single time I just want to practice with a bow and arrow." said Gwen defensively.

After Rachael had finished squeezing Gwen into the pink dress she led her over to a small desk with a mirror and chair and started brushing her hair. "So, your father was telling me about your journey to Morendale earlier today," Rachael said, trying to start another conversation before things got even more awkward.

"He, he did?" Gwen said, suddenly sounding nervous.

"Yes, and I have to say, quite the adventure you two have been on," Rachael said smiling, not noticing Gwen's change in attitude.

"So, so he told you how I ended up in the past?" Gwen said, her face turning a deep shade of red. Rachael heard the change in Gwen's voice that time and saw the look of embarrassment on her face. Rachael could instantly tell what was going on. Gwen was still feeling guilty about causing the whole mess and Rachael had touched a sensitive spot. Immediately Rachael felt guilty for making Gwen upset and quickly apologized.

"Oh I'm sorry," she said, "I should've..."

"I'm fine," Gwen said cutting her off. Rachael could easily tell that Gwen was lying and quickly thought of something that would comfort her.

"Hey look, everything's going to be fine. Don't go beating yourself up, ok?" she said soothingly.

"Yeah, ok," Gwen muttered, still not taking her eyes off the ground.

Rachael put the hairbrush down on the desk and whirled Gwen around and brought her head up so that they were both looking directly into each other's eyes. "Listen, your father told me that the reason he followed you is because he could tell you wanted his help, he's going to help you get through this ok."

"Really?" Gwen said surprised, "He said that?" "Yes, he did," Rachael said smiling. Rachael let Gwen sit there for a moment and soak in what she had said and after a minute of silence Gwen did something Rachael wasn't expecting. Gwen got up and hugged her.

"Thank you," Gwen said. "Thanks for making me feel better." At first Rachael was shocked at what Gwen was doing, but after a moment she hugged her back.

"Don't mention it," she said. The two girls hugged each other for a long time before they broke apart. When they finally did Rachael saw that Gwen had tears in her eyes.

"Now come on," Rachael said as she picked up a pair of pink heels and handed them to Gwen, "We have dinner to attend to."

Rachael turned around and walked towards the door, but before Gwen followed, she smiled and whispered to herself, "Thanks Mom."

Chapter 15

Food and Armor

After I finished changing into the clothes that Rachael had left for me, I flopped down on my bed and waited for Leo to come and get me. It wasn't long before I heard a knocking on my door and Leo walked in. "Are you ready?" he asked. "Yes," I said, getting up. I followed Leo as he led me through the castle to the dining room.

"Aren't we getting Gwen?" I asked him. "Rachael will be bringing Miss Gwen down very soon," Leo answered.

"Oh, ok?" I said, wondering why it was taking Gwen longer to get ready. There was a brief pause between us and for a moment I was afraid there was going to be an awkward silence, but thankfully Leo continued talking. "I saw what you did in the canyon," he said.

"What?" I asked in confusion.

"In the canyon," he explained, "When we found you. You were laying on top of Miss Gwen. You were shielding her."

"Oh yeah, right. That" I said, understanding what he was talking about, "Yeah, I guess that was kind of pointless and stupid, wasn't it?"

"Pointless and stupid?" Leo said raising an eyebrow, "If it was pointless and stupid then why did you do it?"

I stopped and thought for a second before I said, "I guess because it was the only thing I could think of doing."

Leo chuckled to himself and said, "In all my years of being a father I've learned that you'd do anything to help your child, even if it was pointless and stupid."

Leo and I continued walking and as we got near the dining room I started hearing strange sounds coming from somewhere. I listened more closely and as I did, it sounded like some sort of party was going on. For a brief moment I thought about The Annual Royal

Celebration, but this sounded nothing like that. This party sounded upbeat and the people I heard talking sounded like they were actually having fun. As Leo and I got closer to the dining room, the sounds of the party grew louder and louder. By the time Leo and I made it down to the dining room entrance it so loud that I almost couldn't hear myself think.

"Here we are," Leo said pushing open the door.

As soon as the door was opened my jaw dropped. The entire dining room was packed to the brim with people (it seemed like everybody in the entire kingdom was there) and every single one of them looked like they were having a good time. As I looked around the room I couldn't believe my eyes. I saw everything; from people breathing fire to people swallowing swords, to even some people using magic to make fireworks explode periodically throughout the room.

All around the walls of the dining room were tables where people were sitting and enjoying all types of delicious looking food. In the middle of the room was an empty space and unlike The Royal Celebration, people were actually dancing in it. I looked up and saw to my astonishment acrobats hanging from the ceiling, doing tricks that I was sure would make even Gwen jealous. Looking at it all, I was completely awestruck! This, *this happy event*, was what The Royal Celebration should have been.

"I didn't know you were throwing a party for us," I told Leo.

"Party?" Leo asked surprised raising an eyebrow, "What party? This is just supper time." I stared at Leo in disbelief. If this was just supper, I couldn't imagine what a party would be like.

Leo led me through the crowd of people. As we walked, people got out of our way and bowed to Leo as he passed them. Leo nodded to each of them and led me straight to the back of the dining room where the head table was. The head table had 12 chairs at it, and all but four were occupied. Leo sat down in the chair that was directly in the middle next to a woman that I guess was his wife. Leo's wife turned and nodded at me, giving a welcoming smile, and I gave a small bow in respect before I sat down next to Leo. As soon as I was seated servants immediately came over and placed loads of trays on the table in front of us and I continued to be astonished.

I'd thought I'd seen it all when I'd first walked in here, but apparently I was wrong. The servants placed every, *literally every*, kind of food you could imagine in front of us. There were the normal kinds of food like chicken, pork, turkey, fish, potatoes and gravy, every kind of fruit and vegetable, but then there were foods that I had never even seen before, nor could describe. All of it was laid out before me and all of it looked absolutely delicious.

"Dig in," Leo said grabbing some of the food. I didn't argue as I started filling my plate with all the various types of food. Up until that point I didn't know just how hungry I was, but after seeing everything in front of me, I was now practically starving. As I ate I looked over at the two empty chairs next to me and I wondered where Gwen and Rachael were. I continued to wonder that as I ate and I was almost done with my second helping of food when the dining room doors suddenly opened.

I looked up and almost spit my food out in disbelief. Standing there in the doorway was Rachael, wearing a fancy green dress. Shockingly, however, standing next to her, almost completely unrecognizable, was Gwen. Gwen was also wearing a fancy dress, a pink one. Her hair was all brushed and done up making her look, for a lack of a better word, beautiful. Gwen looked incredibly uncomfortable, like she didn't want anyone to notice her. That was impossible though because as soon as the two entered the dining room, the entire room seem to stop and stare at them.

Gwen and Rachael made their way to the head table, Rachael greeting everyone along the way and Gwen doing her best to try and remain as inconspicuous as she possibly could. When the two made it up to the table I stood up and gave a small bow to Rachael.

"You know, you don't have to be so formal," Rachael said giggling.

"Oh right, sorry," I said laughing a bit. I looked behind Rachael and noticed that Gwen had a smug smile on her face. "You look good," I said teasing her.

156

"Shut up," Gwen said dropping her smile. Both Rachael and I laughed. Gwen and Rachael greeted Leo and his wife and after they had greeted them back, I'd thought I'd be polite and got up and pulled out the chair next to me. I had meant for the chair to be for Gwen, but Gwen took one look at it and sat down in the other unoccupied chair. I looked at Gwen in confusion, but she just smiled back at me and said nothing.

"Thank you," Rachael said smiling, sitting down in the chair.

"Oh, you're welcome," I said as I pushed Rachael's chair in and sat back down. I looked over at Gwen and saw that she had the same smug look as before and I wondered why as I started filling my plate up again.

After finishing my third helping of food I finally sat my fork down, feeling completely stuffed, but that was before the servants came over and whisked away all the food dishes and in an instant replaced them with the desert trays. Almost at once I was starving again. Just like the regular food there was almost every kind of dessert imaginable. Cakes, pastries, ice cream; you name it, it was there. Everyone at the table started filling their plates again. While I was eating I looked over at Gwen and noticed that she was stuffing several large chunks of cake in her mouth at once. That was, until she caught Rachael giving her a shocked look. Gwen immediately dropped what she was eating and blushed in embarrassment.

As soon as everyone at the head table was finished with desserts, the servants once again cleared the entire table. I sat back in my chair feeling completely satisfied, watching all the strange sights going on around the dining room. All of a sudden Leo pushed back his chair and stood up, offering his hand to his wife. His wife took it and both of them strolled out to the middle of the room. As soon as they were out on the dance floor, the band started playing a slow, soothing tune. The two started doing a slow dance around the dance floor and as I watched them, I noticed out of the corner of my eye that Gwen was watching me and Rachael with a look of anticipation on her face, almost like she was waiting for something to happen.

"All right, fine!" Gwen suddenly said, making Rachael and I jump. Gwen got up out of her chair, yanked me out of mine, and started dragging me by my shirt towards the dance floor. Behind me I could hear Rachael laughing.

"What are you doing?" I asked as I was dragged along behind her.

"Come on, you owe me a father-daughter dance," Gwen said.

"Wait what!" I said in confusion. Gwen led me down to the dance floor and held out her hand. I hesitated.

"What, don't you know how to slow dance?" she asked.

"No, I've never done it before," I replied. Gwen only rolled her eyes and sighed before grabbing one of my hands and placing the other on her waist which made me blush.

"Then I guess this'll be your first time," she said.

And with that sentence, we were off. Gwen and I spun around the dance floor, slowly dancing to the sweet tune the band was playing. Since I had never slow danced with anyone before, moving around was a little bit awkward. Every once in a while I would accidently step on Gwen's foot but she would let me know that it was ok by stepping on my foot back. This little routine went on for a while until I finally started getting the hang of things. No longer was I stepping on Gwen's feet and Gwen and I had a certain rhythm finally going. As Gwen and I continued spinning around the dance floor I caught brief images of people standing around and watching us. I happened to notice Rachael standing among the crowd, grinning from ear to ear. We passed Leo and his wife dancing and he gave me an approving nod.

Finally the song ended and Gwen and I stopped dancing while the audience watching applauded. Gwen gave me a bow thanking me for the dance and as she did I had a thought. *I had just danced with my own daughter. For me this was our very first dance together.* Thinking about that made me feel strangely old.

"You two were amazing," Rachael said running up to us.

"Thanks," Gwen said smiling at Rachael's comment.

"Wonderful job you two," Leo said walking over, holding his wife's hand. "Thank you sir," I said. "I've come to say goodnight to both of you, I'm off to bed, and you should be too. We have a big day ahead of us tomorrow," Leo said.

"We do?" I asked, confused.

"Yes, tomorrow we have to get you ready for the last part of your journey," he said. After hearing Leo say that I mentally hit myself. I had forgotten how close Gwen and I were to The Time Stone. That meant tomorrow was probably going to be our final day on this crazy journey. Thinking about that made me feel excited, but also incredibly sad at the same time.

"We have to get you ready for the journey, get you some armor..." Leo said.

"Wait, Armor!" Both Gwen and I said at the same time.

"Yes," Leo said smiling, "You'll need some armor, shields, oh and a sword."

"Wait, sword," I whispered.

"Yes," Leo replied. I couldn't believe what I was hearing. Not only was I getting armor, but I was also getting a shield and a sword. As I thought about that I suddenly flashed back to me and my tryout for Cornelius's Royal Guard.

"Well goodnight, you two," Leo said leaving.

Gwen turned around and I saw she was practically beaming. "Isn't this great!" she said, "They're giving us swords and shields."

"Yeah great," I said trying to sound enthusiastic as I remembered the disaster that happened when I was eight.

The next morning the sun was barely over the horizon when I heard a knocking at my door. I slowly rolled off my bed, trudged over, and opened it. Standing there fully dressed were Leo, Rachael, and Gwen.

"Dad come on, why aren't you dressed yet?" Gwen said, shocked.

"It's barely light outside," I said, a little annoyed that I had been woken up so early.

"She's right," Leo said, "We have to get started right away if we want to get to The Time Stone as soon as possible."

I sighed heavily and said, "Give me a minute."

A minute turned out to be ten. I was so tired that it took me a while to pull out my clothes and put them on. After I finally did get dressed, I opened my door again and walked out into the hallway where everyone was still waiting.

"Finally!" Gwen said sarcastically.

"Oh be quiet," I grumbled causing Gwen to snicker. Leo led us through the castle with me dragging my feet as I lagged behind. Leo led us through numerous hallways and staircases until we finally came to a wooden door.

"We go down from here," Leo said. I wondered what he meant by that, but after he opened the wooden door ahead of him, I understood. On the other side of the door was a spiral stone staircase going downwards. The entire group started descending. As we made our way downstairs I couldn't tell how deep we were going (I lost count after stair 542), but I did notice that the deeper we went, the hotter it seemed to get. At first it was just warm, but soon my whole body began to sweat. I looked over at Gwen and I could tell she was hot too, so I knew it wasn't just me.

Finally after who knows how long, the four of us finally reached the bottom of the stairs where another door awaited us. "Where are we, a furnace?" I asked, now feeling like I was going to catch on fire.

"You could say that," Leo said chuckling. Leo pushed the door open and instantly a cloud of heat and smoke hit me, completely drenching me in sweat. When the smoke finally cleared I saw where Leo had led us to.

We were in some sort of forgery. There were about ten furnaces in the stone room and all of them were lit, heating the room up to ridiculously high temperatures. There were ten men in the room, each stationed at his own furnace, all wearing blacksmith gear and tending the fires.

"What is this?" I asked.

"This is the castle forge," Leo said, "This is where we make our weapons and armor."

"But I thought you were sorcerers, not blacksmiths," I said.

Leo laughed, "We are skilled in many areas, including metal forging," he said.

Leo made all the blacksmiths in the forge stop what they were doing and gathered them in the middle of the room. He told them that they were going to help construct the armor and weapons that Gwen and I were going to use on our journey. After that, everyone in the forge got right to work. Rachael came over with a piece of ribbon and started taking Gwen and my measurements. At first this wasn't so bad, but soon Rachael started measuring around places that made me feel slightly uncomfortable. I felt my face turning red and when I looked up I saw Gwen suppressing a fit of laughter.

"You're enjoying this aren't you," I said sarcastically.

"Yes, yes, I am," Gwen smugly replied through her snickering.

"I wouldn't laugh if I were you," Rachael said smiling mischievously, "You're next." Gwen instantly got quiet.

After taking Gwen's measurements (Rachael made sure to make it extra uncomfortable just for me) she gave them to the blacksmiths. Now normally making a full suit of armor for one person, let alone two people, would take forever, but then again the people making our suits weren't normal blacksmiths. Watching the blacksmith's work was unlike anything I'd ever seen. After putting the pieces of metal inside the furnace, the blacksmiths used their magic to make the fire grow to super high temperatures.

A couple seconds later the blacksmith's took the heated metal out of the fire and started forging them into the different parts of the armor. After about 20 minutes of waiting, the blacksmiths had managed to forge not only Gwen and my armor, but also two shields for us as well. Gwen's shield had an image of the manticore we'd fought on it. Looking at it I suddenly felt the pain in my leg again.

My shield had a picture of a phoenix on it. I guessed it was supposed to be Pipsqueak.

Putting the armor on was a difficult challenge for me. Since I had never worn armor in my life I didn't know how to put it on or even which piece went where. Thankfully though Gwen was an expert at putting armor on, managing to put her own on in 5-minutes flat. "Here let me help you," she said walking over, eager to be helping me.

It took over a good 15 minutes, but eventually Gwen and I (but mostly Gwen) managed to get me into my new suit of armor and I had to say, I really liked how it felt. At first I thought that because of my size the armor would be big and bulky on me, but the suit was slim and lightweight.

"Comfortable," I said with surprise and gratitude.

"Those armors and shields are made by the best blacksmith's in Morendale," Leo said, "It's nearly indestructible and completely fireproof. It can even withstand any type of magic there is, so Tharon won't be able to harm you while you're wearing it."

"Great!" I said enthusiastically.

"But you can still die if you get hit in the head or fall from a high place or something like that," Rachael said cautiously.

"Oh. Not great," I said less enthusiastically.

"So are we ready or not?" Gwen said impatiently.

"Almost," Leo said, "There's just one thing left to do."

That one thing left to do turned out to be a sword. Leo banged his walking stick on the floor and a couple of the blacksmiths brought over a large wooden chest. Inside the chest were all sort of different weapons. Swords, daggers, bows and arrows; you name it, it was all there.

"You'll need a weapon just in case the worst happens," Leo said, "Pick whatever one you want."

Gwen looked at all the weapons with a twinkle in her eye and immediately started digging through the chest. After about ten seconds of searching she pulled out a sword that was about 2 feet in length. "Yep this will do," Gwen said looking at it. After Gwen had

162

found her sword she stepped back letting me know that it was my turn. I looked at the chest full of weapons and gulped. I flashed back to when I was eight-years-old and how I wasn't able to hold any of the weapons back then. I was sure nothing was different now.

I slowly approached the chest and started digging through and as I expected nothing seemed to work. Every single weapon I tried out was either too big or too heavy for me to use. As I dug through, I became increasingly nervous. I could feel everyone in the room watching me and I knew that I had been digging through the chest for several long minutes. I needed to find a weapon and soon. However as I threw the last weapon back into the chest and wondered what I was going to do Leo suddenly spoke up.

"You can't find a weapon that works for you?" he asked me. I turned around and faced him and shook my head no. Leo didn't even think twice before he said, "Well then, I guess we'll just have to make a sword that fits you."

I had no idea what Leo was talking about but Leo suddenly turned around and started a fire in one of the furnaces again. I then watched in amazement as Leo himself pulled a piece of metal out of the fire and started forging it. After waiting for a couple of minutes, Leo turned around and in his hand was a gleaming new sword.

The sword wasn't very impressive looking, in fact in looked kind of plain. It was shorter than the sword Gwen chose, only about a foot long, and it had a golden colored hilt. Leo handed it to me and I hesitated taking it, fearing the exact same outcome. However, as soon as I took it, the sword felt completely right in my hands. It wasn't too light or too heavy. It was the right length it needed to be and fit in my hand perfectly. This sword was perfect.

I turned around and saw Gwen looking at the sword with wide eyes. "What?" I asked her. Suddenly Leo stuck his hand out again like he was asking for the sword back.

"And now the last thing we need to do is give it a name," he said.

"A name?" I said confused handing the sword back to him.

"Yes," he said, "every great sword has had a name." I couldn't help but smile as I Immediately started to think of all kinds of cool names to call my new sword. Backbreaker, jaw ripper, spline crusher.

But before I could say anything, Gwen suddenly said, "Kit."

"Kit?" I said turning around. "Yeah that's your sword's name," she said.

"I'm not naming my sword Kit," I said.

"Look," Gwen said, "That's the sword you have in the future, and in the future you call it Kit."

"Why would I name my sword Kit?" I asked. Gwen just shrugged but suddenly Leo chuckled behind me.

"Well then," he said, "Kit it is."

"Wait, you're listening to her?" I asked turning around.

"Yes," Leo said smiling. Leo turned around and after a minute of waiting, he handed the sword back to me and I saw etched into the blade the letters K, I, and T. "Now then," Leo said, "let's get going."

Later that afternoon Gwen and I were sitting on two horses that Leo had provided us with on the edge of Morendale. Behind us were a group of twenty guards who would be accompanying us to the mountain where The Time Stone was. The plan we had come up with was that Gwen and I would ride to the mountain, get The Time Stone, and bring it back, so we could use it to get Gwen home.

We didn't know exactly how we were going to defeat Tharon, but Leo said keeping the stone safe was our number one priority. Right then we were waiting for Leo to bring us something that he said we were going to need.

As we waited, a large group of people had gathered to stand and watch us, and it made me feel slightly uncomfortable. Pipsqueak chirped happily on my shoulder which was now possible thanks to my armor being fireproof.

"Are you ready?" I suddenly heard Leo say. I turned around and saw Leo and Rachael walking towards us. Everyone in the crowd and all the guards bowed in respect. I saw that Leo had a scroll in his hand along with a bag. "As ready as I'll ever be." I replied. Leo handed me the bag.

"This should help you get The Time Stone," he said. I took the bag and looked at the mountain we were headed to.

"Do you think it's still safe?" I asked.

"Yes," Leo said looking mournfully at the mountain, "But if we don't act fast Tharon will seize the stone and after that it's all over."

"What will happen if he gets the stone?" I asked.

"He would most likely use it to go back and time and destroy Morendale out of revenge. After that he would probably use it to make himself a god and rule all of humanity." I shuddered at the thought of Tharon being in control of everything.

"Why don't you come with us?" I asked Leo. He smiled as he showed me the scroll in his hands. I received word from one of my top guardsmen, they found some more people out in The Wasteland and they are bringing them here. They will be here shortly and I have to be here to greet them." I sat there confused by the news.

"Wait, what do you mean you found more people in The Wasteland?" I asked. Leo only chuckled. "Don't worry," he said, "You'll meet them soon enough, but right now focus on getting The Time Stone."

"Ready," Gwen said walking her horse over to me. Gwen was busy saying goodbye to Rachael and I could see a hint of tears in her eyes for some strange reason.

"Well then," Rachael said walking up to me, "I guess I'll see you hopefully by tomorrow."

"Yes, and thank you, for everything," I said giving a small bow.

Rachael giggled, "My pleasure." I saw out of the corner of my eye Gwen smiling happily.

"We're ready," The head guardsmen shouted.

"All right then," I said turning my horse towards the direction of the lone mountain, "Let's go." Everyone started out single file as we started off towards the mountain. As we rode, I moved up next to Gwen, pulled out Kit, and looked at it.

"You know I have no idea how to use this thing don't you?" I said sarcastically.

Gwen laughed and said, "Don't worry Dad, I'll teach you."

Chapter 16

The Journey comes to an End, sort of

For days Tamina and Stewart traveled with the group of soldiers, and during that time very little had actually been explained to them. The leader of the soldiers was very limited in the questions that he answered. The only for-sure thing that Tamina and Stewart knew was that they were headed to a kingdom called Morendale, and that when they got there a person named King Leo would answer all of their questions. So without definite answers for either of them, Tamina and Stewart had to ride in silence, both wondering where exactly they were headed.

After a few days of traveling the entire group finally came to a huge canyon and the leader of the group made everyone stop for the night. "It's dangerous to cross at night, we'll have to wait until morning," he told Tamina as they set up camp. When morning came the leader of the group took everyone along the edge of the canyon until they found a pathway that led down to the bottom that was large enough for their horses.

The group descended into the canyon and as they crossed the bottom Tamina noticed dozens of giant rock piles scattered around the ground. Tamina was about to ask what all the piles were, but when she looked over at the leader she saw that he and all the other soldiers were eying the rock piles suspiciously, almost like they were expecting them to get up and start attacking.

After climbing out of the canyon the group took off again towards a couple of mountains in the distance. As they slowly approached the snowy mountains, both Tamina and Stewart started getting a little nervous, wondering if they were going to have to climb over them. Luckily though, the soldiers led them around the base of the mountains to a secret pass that went straight through them to the other side.

After the group made it through the pass both Tamina and Stewart started looking around for Morendale, however all they saw in front of them were open fields and another mountain far off in the distance.

"Where's Morendale?" Tamina asked.

"Not far," the leader of the group said, "We will be there soon."

Tamina heard Stewart groan behind her and she couldn't blame him. They had been traveling for days, all they wanted now was to get to this "Morendale" place they had been told about.

"How far away is this Morendale?" Stewart asked, annoyed.

The leader of the group calmly answered Stewart's question by pointing and saying, "Not far." Tamina and Stewart looked over to where the leader was pointing and together they saw what looked like a small kingdom. Both of them were stunned to actually see a kingdom all the way out here and Tamina was about to ask why it was out in the middle of nowhere, but the leader of the group abruptly said, "Let's go," and all of them took off again.

It took the group just a few short hours for them to ride from the mountains to Morendale. When they finally arrived the leader went up to the soldier stationed at the main gate and told him to go inform King Leo that they had arrived. The soldier saluted in respect then opened the gate for the group before he went riding off towards the castle. The leader led Tamina and Stewart through Morendale's gate and as they entered the kingdom, they couldn't help but be completely speechless from what they saw.

Morendale was unlike anything they had ever seen before. The architecture of buildings in the village alone were beyond beautiful. Tamina looked up and gasped as she saw a gleaming white castle towering above them. All her life Tamina and the rest of the world believed that her father's castle was the most magnificent castle in the entire world, but Morendale's castle put her father's castle to shame.

The leader of the group turned around and addressed the rest of the soldiers. "You are all dismissed," he said to them. The soldiers saluted him and rode off leaving only the leader, Tamina, and Stewart. "This way," he said turning back around and gesturing for the two of them to follow. The leader continued making his way through Morendale's village towards the castle, Tamina and Stewart following right behind him.

"Where are we going?" Tamina asked him.

"I'm taking you up to the castle. King Leo is expecting you," he replied.

"Wait, the king's expecting us?" Stewart said surprised.

"Yes," the leader said nodding his head, "After we found you two I sent him a letter saying we were bringing you here. I'm taking you to meet him so he can explain everything to you both."

"Even about Sam?" Tamina asked.

"Yes, he will tell you what you want to know about the boy you're looking for," he said nodding his head. Tamina breathed a sigh of relief. She was finally going to see Sam again. They had finally made it. As they rode towards the castle Tamina's mind began to race as she thought about all the things she was going to say to Sam once they were reunited.

The three of them rode through the village until they stopped at the castle's front doors. The three of them dismounted their horses and the leader whistled and a couple of groundskeepers came bustling towards them.

"Take the horses to the stables and give them some water," he said to them. The groundskeepers bowed in respect before taking the horse's reins from Tamina and Stewart and leading them off.

Once the three of them were alone again the leader turned around and pushed open the castle's front doors and stepped inside. Tamina and Stewart followed him and once they were inside they were again absolutely speechless. They had stepped inside the castle's entry way and just like the outside of the castle, it was completely breathtaking. Everything, from the floor to the ceiling had a regal feel to it that was unmatched by anything Tamina and Stewart had ever seen before. Tamina and Stewart in fact were *so* caught up by the way the castle looked that they didn't even notice the two people standing in the hall.

"Do you like it?" they suddenly heard. Tamina and Stewart whirled around and saw a man with grey hair and beard carrying a walking stick and a girl of about Sam's age standing there watching them patiently.

"Oh, sorry," Tamina said a little embarrassed, "you must be King Leo, right?"

The man and girl walked up to them and dismissed the leader before the man spoke to them, "Yes, I am King Leo," he said nodding his head, "and this is my daughter, Princess Rachael." Both Tamina and Stewart bowed in respect.

"We're sorry for intruding your Majesty, it just that we're looking for someone and we heard that he was here," Tamina said jumping right away into why Stewart and she were here.

Leo chuckled and said, "A little impatient isn't she," addressing Stewart.

"Um, a little," Stewart said cautiously. Tamina shot Stewart an annoyed look and Stewart pointed his eyes down at the ground, his cheeks turning red. Leo chuckled and turned back to Tamina.

"You must be Princess Tamina and Sir Stewart, correct?"

Both Tamina and Stewart looked at Leo in shock. "Ye…Yes," Tamina said, "How did you know our names?"

"Sam told us who you are," Rachael answered.

As soon as Tamina heard Sam's name mentioned she completely lost it again. "Sam's here! I knew it! Where is he? Is he ok? Can I see him now?" Tamina yelled excitedly.

Rachael jumped back in alarm and Stewart lost all the color in his face. "Tamina!" he said sharply. Tamina stopped and suddenly realized what she had just done and her face turned a dark shade of red. "Sorry, sorry," she quickly said, incredibly embarrassed at her outburst, "it's just that, we wanted to know where he is. Can you take us to him?"

Leo seemed to be the only one not affected by Tamina's screaming as he never dropped his patient gaze. "Sam is not here," he calmly said.

"What!" Tamina and Stewart said together in disbelief, "But I thought you said..." Tamina started to say.

"Sam was here, but he has left," Leo explained. Tamina couldn't believe it. They had come all this way and once again Sam was nowhere to be seen. Tamina's breath became shallow as she felt tears starting to form in her eyes.

"Now, now my dear, don't cry," Leo said coming up to Tamina and comforting her, "Sam is not here, but I promise he'll return soon enough."

Tamina sniffed before she said, "Wh...what are you talking about? Where is Sam?" "Come, let us walk," Leo said turning around and motioning for Tamina and Stewart to follow him, "You need answers, and I am willing to give them."

By the time Leo had finished explaining everything to Tamina and Stewart, both of their brains had completely stopped working. It was too much for them to handle. Leo had told them a ridiculous story about how Sam's daughter from the future had accidently come back in time while also releasing an evil king, and that Sam and his daughter were on their way to stop the king from getting his hands on The Time Stone from the bedtime stories Tamina used to read to him.

As Tamina and Stewart were told all of this, only one thing went through both their minds. *These people were absolutely insane.* Never once during the story did they believe it, but it wasn't until the part where Leo was explaining how they were supposedly sorcerers where Stewart finally spoke up. He angrily told him that there was no way what he was telling them was true and that they needed to know where Sam was right now or else he and Tamina were leaving.

Instead of responding to Stewart, Leo and Rachael instead looked at each other before both of them stuck out their right hands and made fire erupt out of their palms. Tamina and Stewart jumped back in horror and awe. They watched in disbelief as both Leo and Rachael made the fire dance around, making it do all sorts of different tricks.

After they had extinguished the fire Leo asked if they believed him now, but Tamina and Stewart were in so much disbelief that they couldn't even respond. Leo smiled at their shocked expressions and went back to telling his story. When he had finished telling them everything, Tamina was so bewildered that she literally felt like she was going to pass out.

"So, the girl we've been hearing about is Sam's daughter?" Tamina asked in a whisper that was barely audible.

"Everything I have told you is true," Leo said nodding his head. Tamina felt herself sinking to the ground, unable to believe what she had just saw and heard. In one twenty minute period her entire world had been completely uprooted and turned upside down.

"Wait a minute," Stewart said, "You mean that there's this, Lord Tharon guy out there, and you sent Sam and his...his daughter out there to go stop him from getting a stone?"

"Both of them were willing to retrieve The Time Stone for me," Leo said.

"But you said Tharon was dangerous, and you sent them out alone?" Stewart said angrily.

"I did not send them out alone. I sent guards to protect them. I promise you that he'll return safely." Stewart didn't know how to react properly. Instead he, like Tamina, found himself sinking to the floor, feeling the exact same way she did; not truly believing what Leo said about Sam returning home safely.

Our ride to The Time Stone actually turned out to be a pretty enjoyable one. Gwen and I took the lead as the twenty guards who were sent to protect us followed behind. During our time riding I pulled out Kit and Gwen started teaching me how to use it. At first it was a little difficult, especially since I was riding on the back of a horse, but after an hour of practice I started to get the hang of things.

"There, perfect!" Gwen said smiling after I had executed a jab that was giving me troubles.

"All thanks to my great teacher," I said smiling. After I'd said that Gwen gave me a look like she suddenly had realized something before she burst out laughing.

"What?" I asked confused. Gwen calmed down from laughing long enough to say, "It's just that, I learned all my sword skills from you, and now you're learning all your swords skills from me." Gwen went back to laughing as I thought about her statement and when I had fully processed it, I couldn't help but laugh too.

Gwen and I continued my sword training all the way until we reached the base of the mountain. When we finally arrived the sun had sunk below the horizon.

"All right, so how do we get up to the top?" I asked wondering how we were going to get to The Time Stone. Thankfully the guards answered my question as they led Gwen and me over to a spot where a narrow pathway, just large enough where a single horse could walk on, led up the mountain. One-by-one, each of us started going up the narrow pathway. Gwen volunteered to go first, followed by me and Pipsqueak, and then the rest of the guards. As we climbed I would sometimes hear rock shift beneath the horse's hooves and I would grip my horse's reins tighter; desperately hoping that the ground wouldn't suddenly cave beneath me and send me tumbling down the mountainside.

After about an hour or so of climbing our entire group finally reached a part of the mountain were the path stopped and leveled out into a large flat area where a smooth rock wall lay off to the left of us. Everyone dismounted their horses and walked over to the rock wall.

"Well this is where the path ends," Gwen said.

"So where's the stone?" I asked looking around.

"The Time Stone is hidden," One of the guards said, "You must open the door to retrieve it." I had no idea what he meant by that, but I suddenly remembered the bag that Leo handed to me right before we left and thought it might have something in it that might provide a clue or help. I went over to my horse and pulled out the bag and opened it. Inside was a golden medallion with a diamond shape etched into it. Looking at the medallion I had no idea how this was going to open the door to The Time Stone but I suddenly thought that maybe it was a key and that you were supposed to place it in a hole or something.

I went back to the rock wall and started looking around for something that looked like the medallion might fit into. After about 10 minutes of searching I finally found it. Hidden behind a large boulder, almost invisible in the dark, was a round groove that match the size and shape of the medallion perfectly.

I took the medallion and with a little force managed to jam it into the hole. Almost immediately the ground began to shake violently as the medallion's edges lit up bright blue. Pipsqueak squawked in fear and took off from my shoulder as the horses whined in distressed and everyone stumbled around. "Earthquake!" Gwen yelled. I almost believed her as I heard a noise that sounded like the earth was being ripped open, however, as soon as the shaking had started it stopped.

I turned around and saw that a crack had appeared in the stone wall. The crack wasn't very big, it looked just wide enough for an average sized man to fit through. I knew that this was it and saw that Gwen too had the same expression as me--determination. She gave me an approving nod and I made my way over to the crack, but before I got there Pipsqueak came shooting out of the sky and zipped his way inside. I made my way up to the crack and started feeling along the edges. I took a couple of deep breaths, shot one last look at Gwen who nodded her head again, and pushed my way through.

Getting through the crack wasn't a problem for me at all, but then again I was smaller than most people. After I'd entered the crack, I came out into a huge cavern. The first thing that I noticed about the cavern was that it was dark. Or at least it would've been if it wasn't for Pipsqueak who was flying around chirping happily lighting everything up. The next thing I noticed was that the cavern

174

looked more like a cave than an actual chamber. There wasn't anything special about it; no pillars no archways, nothing significant about it except...

Right in the very center of the cavern was a pedestal. And on top of the pedestal being illuminated by the light of Pipsqueak, was The Time Stone. When I first saw The Time Stone I almost couldn't believe it. Instead of looking like an actual stone it looked more like a diamond. The stone was glass-like, and had a blue color to it that made it cast a light-blue shadow on the walls of the cavern.

I stared at the stone, unable to believe we had actually made it. After everything: the bar, the Manticore, the Rock Giants, Tharon, we had finally made it. I was so mesmerized by the stone that I didn't hear Gwen or any of the other guards slip their way through the crack behind me.

"Dad, are you ok?" Gwen asked. I didn't answer, instead I turned her head towards The Time Stone and as soon as she saw it, she whispered, "We, we did it," Gwen whispered. "We did it," I repeated with satisfaction and relief.

"Men secure the door," I heard one of the guards say behind us. After we had stared at the stone for a while, Gwen and I looked at each other and saw that we were both ready to go for it.

We both nodded and slowly approached the pedestal. As we got closer I wondered whether anything was going to happen if we took the stone off the pedestal. *No, Leo and the guards would've told us if something dangerous was going to happen,* I told myself. When Gwen and I were right next to the pedestal we both looked at each other, both wondering if the other person was going to take the stone or not.

"I'll do it," I said. Gwen nodded and I slowly started reaching for the stone, still wondering what was going to happen when I took it. However, before I could grab the stone, there was a loud, rasping, bone-chilling laughter that filled the entire room. Everyone in the room froze as Gwen and I shot each other panicked looks.

"No," I thought, "Please not now," I prayed.

"Well, well…" a deep raspy voice that sent chills through my spine said, "Look who survived."

Chapter 17

A Battle to Save My Life...and the Rest of the World

The air in the cavern was completely sucked out with that sentence. I stood there, my hand outstretched, mere inches away from The Time Stone, completely frozen in terror. I didn't want to believe it, it just couldn't be possible. We had come all this way, had made it this far; and at the very last second, right when we were about to complete our goal...

I looked over at Gwen and saw that she had turned around, a look of fear on her face. There was another bone-chilling laugh and I knew that it was really happening. Even though Gwen and I had prepared for this to happen, I still had hoped that the universe would finally give us a break. But no, not today. I stood there, staring down at The Time Stone, knowing that sooner or later I would have to face reality. Slowly I lowered my arm and, dreading what was to come, turned around to face *him*.

Tharon was standing at the entrance of the cavern smiling at us. Or at least I think he would've been smiling at us if he actually had a mouth. "Hello there," Tharon said.

All the guards immediately went for their weapons, but before any of them could even touch the hilts of their swords Tharon shot blasts of energy at them. All the guards went flying into the cavern walls and slid to the ground where they remained there, motionless. This left only me, Gwen, and Tharon as the only people in the cavern still standing. I looked up at the ceiling and saw that Pipsqueak was flying around in a corner, cowering in fear from Tharon.

"Now is that any way to treat a guest?" Tharon asked one of the guard's lifeless bodies. After a moment of suspenseful silence Tharon said, "Of course not," before he turned his attention back to the two of us. Gwen and I stood there paralyzed with fear. "Well isn't this surprising," he said, slowly moving towards us, "I thought you two would've drowned in that river. I'm impressed. Especially with you," Tharon said addressing me.

With any other person I would've been insulted by his last comment, but Tharon was so terrifying that all I could manage to say was, "H...how did you find us?"

"Oh I've been here for days now," Tharon said, "I would've had The Time Stone by now, but unfortunately I couldn't break the stone's stupid defenses. I knew somebody would eventually come up here to check on it though, so I hid myself and waited patiently for somebody to show up. I never thought it would be you two."

Tharon walked up to Gwen and me, and both of us backed up as far as we could go, right next to the pedestal.

"And now that we have our formalities out of the way," Tharon said stopping a few feet away from us, "I believe you two are standing between me and something that is rightfully mine. So if you would please move out of the way, I'll take the stone and I'll happily let you be on your way."

I was so stricken with fear that I couldn't even respond. However, I suddenly felt a hand grasped my own and I looked down to see Gwen holding my hand. I looked up at Gwen and saw that she was giving me a pleading look as if to tell me, "Don't give it to him."

Seeing her giving me that look made me work up the courage to say, "We'll...never...let...you...get...the...stone."

Gwen smiled proudly at me and I couldn't help but smile back. Our happy little moment didn't last very long though as there was a thunderous BOOM, and Tharon hit us with the same energy as the guards making us to go flying. Thankfully the armor we were wearing protected us from the energy blast so getting hit by it didn't hurt. What *did* hurt was us slamming against the back wall of the cavern.

The pain of hitting the rock wall wasn't as bad as when I fell off the side of the canyon, but it still hurt enough that I couldn't move. "Brave words," I heard Tharon say, "Stupid, but brave."

I painfully forced my head to look up and I saw that Tharon was standing right next to The Time Stone. *No*, I thought as Tharon looked at the stone with wide eyes.

"Finally," I heard him whisper. Tharon started reaching his arm out towards The Time Stone and as he did time seemed to slow down almost to a standstill.

I knew I had to do something. I looked around the cave, desperately trying to locate anything that could help us. That's when I noticed Pipsqueak, still flying up around in the corner. Looking at him I made a split-second decision.

I managed to yell three words using all the energy I had left. I yelled, "Pipsqueak, the stone!"

If the last second had gone by super slowly, the next second went by blazingly fast. Pipsqueak heard me and the small bird went diving out of the air. In a fraction of a second he had grabbed The Time Stone with his talons and taken off out the entrance. I sighed in relief as I watched the phoenix go. I didn't know if he knew to take it to Leo, but at the moment I was just glad that we had managed to keep the stone out of Tharon's hands.

"NO!" Tharon yelled in rage as he tried to shoot the small bird out of the sky, but by then it was too late. Pipsqueak was gone. Tharon whirled around and I saw the sheer anger in his eye holes. "You two will pay for what you have done!" he yelled.

"Go ahead; kill us," Gwen said pushing herself up, "but you'll never get your hands on that stone."

"No," Tharon said in the most menacing voice I had ever heard, "I'm not going to kill you two, not yet anyway," he said. "There are far worse punishments than death." The word death echoed around the cavern and I shuddered as I thought about what could possibly be worse than death.

"Then what are you going to do with us?" Gwen asked. Tharon turned around and started walking back towards the cavern's entrance.

"I am going to make those wretched sorcerers suffer for what they did to me," he said, "and you two will suffer with them."

"But you don't have The Time Stone. What can you do without it?" Gwen spat at him.

Tharon stopped dead in his tracks and turned back around and the threatening tone of his words sent chills down my spine.

"Oh you'll see my dear," We heard him promise.

And see we did, because at that very moment the most terrifying thing that I saw on the entire journey (and that's saying something) happened. Tharon closed his eyes and I could tell he was concentrating hard. At first nothing happened but that soon changed as all the air in the room was sucked out and every shadow (including Gwen and mine's) started slithering towards Tharon. At first I was scared he was going to create more shadow wolves like before, but I was even more horrified when I saw the shadows merging with Tharon, causing him to change.

Gwen and I watched in horror as Tharon's body began to grow and morph. His head changed into the shape of a lizard and his neck became five times longer. His eyes became slits, both his feet and his hands grew long sharp talons and a tail grew out of his back and spines grew from his head all the way down to his tail. And to top things off, out of his back popped two, gigantic, razor-sharp wings. When it was all over, where Tharon once stood, now stood a gigantic black dragon that was so large, it filled the entire cavern.

Gwen and I looked at Tharon in horror, both of us completely petrified. Tharon let out a deep, low, menacing laugh that shook the entire cavern and caused several chunks of the ceiling to fall, narrowly missing Gwen and me.

"You'll see," Tharon said. Tharon started reaching one of his massive claws at us. Gwen and I both tried to get up and make a run for it, but it was useless. Tharon reached out and grabbed both of us in his claws.

Immediately everything went dark. I don't mean that I passed out again, I mean that literally everything went dark; I couldn't see a thing. The only thing that I could see was the faint outline of Gwen and that was it. I heard Tharon let out a thunderous roar which made both Gwen and I vibrate, then I heard a loud noise that sounded like rocks being crushed and I knew that Tharon was breaking his way out of the cavern.

180

After the sound of smashing rocks had died down there was a brief moment where nothing happened and then suddenly I had the feeling of weightlessness, like I was being lifted up in the air.

"He's taking off," Gwen said.

"Where's he going?" I asked.

"Where else," Gwen answered, "Morendale."

And indeed Gwen was right. After 10 minutes of listening to nothing but the sound of the wind whistling by us, Gwen and I started hearing a horrible sound. It was the sound of people shouting and screaming mixed with what sounded like arrows whooshing past us. I heard Tharon let out a thunderous roar and I heard what sounded like bellowing fire followed by more screaming and buildings collapsing.

Gwen and I hung suspended, completely still, listening desperately to the unseen carnage that was happening to Morendale's village, both of us completely shocked as we imagined the destruction that was happening.

Suddenly there was a tremendous CRASH, and Gwen and I were thrown forward in Tharon's claw.

"What happened?" I asked.

"We hit something," Gwen said.

"What?" I asked. Almost instantly I got my answer as there was the sound of a door being thrown open followed by more screaming and the voice of Leo. Gwen and I looked at each other and we both knew that Tharon had forced his way into Morendale's castle.

"Lord Tharon," I heard Leo said.

Tharon let out another deep laugh before he said, "you would be the king of Morendale, I presume."

"I am King Leo. And you, monster have no business being here," I heard Leo said. I heard more shouting followed by several thuds of people hitting the floor, followed by Tharon laughing again.

"Is this the best your guards can do? I must say Your Highness, Morendale's gone downhill since I was last here. Now you have something that belongs to me, hand it over." There was a loud squawk and I recognized it as Pipsqueak, he had made it to Leo.

181

"You will receive nothing!" Leo shouted.

"Wise words from somebody who sends two children to retrieve The Time Stone," Tharon said coldly.

I then heard something that made my heart stop. "What have you done to Sam?" I heard a girl shout. *No*, I thought, *it can't be.* Tharon let out another laugh that shook the whole room before he suddenly chucked Gwen and me at the ground. Hitting the tile floor wasn't as bad as hitting the cavern wall, but it did still feel like a couple of my bones had snapped.

"Sam!" I heard several people scream and I froze again in complete shock as I recognized one of the voices. *Please, don't let it be her, not now*, I thought as I pushed myself up off the ground. I looked up at the people standing in front of me, and indeed my fears were true.

Standing there right above me were four people: Rachael, Leo (who had Pipsqueak on his shoulder), and Stewart. The fourth figure was at the very front, with her eyes wide with concern, looking incredibly tired and worn. "Ta...Tamina?" I said in disbelief.

Tamina suddenly shouted, "LOOK OUT!" before I found myself being yanked up off the ground by Gwen as Tharon opened his mouth and shot fire at us.

"TAKE COVER, GO!" Leo yelled. Everyone besides Leo and Stewart dived behind a fallen pillar leaving Leo and Stewart to fight Tharon.

Stewart deflected the bolts of energy that Tharon launched at them and Leo used his walking stick to cast his own energy at Tharon, but looking at them I could tell it was useless. Stewart's shield wasn't able to stand against the energy that Tharon shot and Leo's energy bolts weren't damaging Tharon at all. When more guards rushed in to help, Tharon simply shot bolts of energy at them as soon as they entered the room, causing them to go flying away like ragdolls.

"Is this what Morendale's become? Pathetic," Tharon laughed, "Come on, give me an actual challenge."

"Any suggestions?" I asked as we watched the horror unfolding before us.

"Tharon's not going to stop until he gets his hands on this," Rachael said opening her hands and revealing The Time Stone.

Tamina gasped and said, "So that's…"

"Yes, this is The Time Stone," Rachael said.

Tamina's mouth fell open as she turned and looked at Gwen and slowly started to say, "So, your, really…" before there was a loud, BOOM, and part of the wall behind us exploded as Tharon shot another ball of energy.

"Um, Tamina," I said as I uncovered my face, "I don't think now's the best time to be discussing this."

"Agreed," Gwen said before she unsheathed her sword, "we need to be helping them."

Gwen went to stand up, but Rachael quickly said, "No!" and immediately pulled her back to the ground.

"What?" Gwen said a little annoyed, "they need our help."

"You'd be committing suicide. Look," Rachael said looking over the pillar.

Everyone looked over the pillar again and saw what Rachael was talking about. Both Stewart and Leo looked to be on the verge of collapse from their fight against Tharon's attacks.

"Ok, let's recap," I said ducking behind the pillar, "We have a thousand year old king made entirely out of shadows who seems to be invincible. Nothing seems to faze him. Are you sure there isn't *anything* we can use to destroy him before he brutally murders all of us?" I asked Rachael desperately.

She looked down at the ground and I could tell she was thinking hard. Meanwhile more walls in the room exploded around us as Tharon continued his attack.

Finally Rachael said, "Wait, I think I remember my father saying that since Tharon's made up of pure shadows, natural sunlight can harm him."

"Great!" I said, ecstatic that we had found Tharon's weakness, "So all we have to do is keep him busy until sunrise."

"Uh, Sam," Tamina said looking over the pillar, "I don't think we have that kind of time." I looked over the pillar again and saw that both Leo and Stewart were now barely managing to dodge Tharon's energy blasts.

"And besides," Rachael said, "Even if the sun does come up soon, all Tharon would have to do is find a dark spot to hide in until night falls."

"Then what do we do?" I asked hopelessly.

"We lead him out into the open," Gwen said. Everyone turned towards Gwen.

"What?" I asked her.

"We lead Tharon out into the open so that when the sun rises he has no place to hide," she said.

"Great," I said, "Just one problem, where exactly are we going to lead him to?"

"The roof," Rachael suddenly said.

"The roof?" the rest of us asked in confusion turning towards Rachael.

Rachael nodded her head, "The castle roof, There are no dark places Tharon could hide in up there. He'd be completely exposed." I thought over this plan. Looking at it on the surface I could tell it was very flawed, definitely made up on the spot, and there were a lot of things that could go wrong. A lot. However, it was the only plan that we had.

"Let's do it," I said.

"Ok then," Gwen said standing up, "I'll lead Tharon up to the roof then."

"What!" I said as Gwen moved over to Rachael and asked her for The Time Stone, "Are you insane!"

"You already know the answer to that Dad," Gwen said chuckling.

Gwen started to walk away, but before she walked out into the open I stood up, drew Kit and said, "Then I'm coming with you."

"Sam no!" Tamina said terrified as she quickly grabbed my arm before I could follow Gwen. I looked down at Tamina and saw the pleading horror in her eyes and it made me pause for a second. Tamina and Stewart had come all this way themselves to look for me; *me*. And here I was, going off to probably get myself killed.

Looking at her I knew that if I made it through this I was going to have a very long conversation with her, but right now there were other things that needed to be done, so all I said was, "Tamina, I've got to do this. My daughter needs me."

Tamina looked around the room and I could tell she was desperately trying to think of something to talk me out of this. "Sam this ridiculous. This is insane. This is stupid," she said.

I chuckled at the last part of her sentence and said, "Well, I learned that a parent will always do something stupid when it comes to helping their kid. Isn't that right, Mom?"

Upon hearing the word *Mom*, Tamina went ridged as her eyes became wide and she let go of my arm. Tamina sat there staring off into space. I looked over at Rachael and saw she was smiling with small tears in her eyes. I turned around and followed Gwen who was also smiling.

I thought Gwen was going to say something to me about what I'd just said, but all she said was, "Are you ready?" I nodded my head as I got Kit ready.

Gwen and I stepped out from behind the pillar and into the open. Leo and Stewart were still battling Tharon and from the looks of it they had probably another 30 seconds before they would be done for altogether. Gwen and I slowly moved over to the door and opened it so that we could immediately dash out.

After that I took one deep breath and silently prayed that nothing too painful was going to happen to us before shouting, "Hey Tharon..!"

A hush fell over the entire room. Both Leo and Stewart stopped fighting and looked behind them. Unfortunately, that proved to be an unwise decision as Tharon took the opportunity to send another bolt of energy at them. Both of them went flying across the room and crashed into the walls. I heard Rachael and Tamina scream and Pipsqueak squawk in fright. I watched in fear as the two men slid to

185

the ground and remained there unmoving. I turned back to Tharon and saw that he was glaring at us. I opened my mouth to say something, but I was so scared I couldn't get any words out of my mouth. Thankfully though Gwen was kind enough to finish my sentence for me. And she said probably *the worst possible thing imaginable to taunt him.*

"You want this stone," Gwen yelled holding The Time Stone above her head, "You can have it when you pry it from our cold, lifeless corpses."

"What!" I screamed at Gwen, completely terrified by her word choice.

"I can wait five minutes," Tharon growled at us. Tharon started to open his mouth and I knew he was going to throw another energy blast at us.

Gwen suddenly shouted, "Don't just stand there, RUN!" Both of us took off towards the door and out of the room. Tharon shot at us, but luckily Gwen and I were far enough away that we managed to dodge his blast. As Gwen and I ran off down the hall I turned back and saw that instead of directly chasing us, Tharon was melting back into the shadows.

Gwen and I ran through the halls of Morendale's castle, not knowing where exactly we were or where we were supposed to go. All we knew was we had to get to the roof, so anytime Gwen and I came across a staircase that went up we took it, not caring where it led. Every once in a while either Gwen or I would turn around to see if Tharon was following right behind us. Although we never saw him, both of us knew that he was still always there, chasing us by silently moving through the shadows.

Eventually after running for a long, long time, Gwen and I managed to make it to the top floor of the castle. As we ran through the halls Gwen started kicking room doors open until she finally said, "Quick, in here." She pulled me inside what looked to be a bedroom then quickly slammed the door shut. She then got out her sword and chucked it at the window on the opposite side of the room, shattering it. "Come on," she said. I followed her as both of us climbed out of the window and onto the castle roof.

The first two things that I noticed was one: it was still dark outside, and two: we were incredibly high up. Looking down at Morendale's village made me feel lightheaded. I knew that one wrong step and it would be a very long, very painful fall.

"Great," I said as Gwen and I carefully moved across the roof, "Now what?"

"Now, we distract him long enough for the sun to come up," Gwen said.

"Great," I said sighing, looking over at the mountains in the east. Just behind them were rays of light that told me that the sun was coming up. However I knew the chances of Gwen and I holding Tharon off long enough for the sun to rise were practically zero.

Suddenly we heard Tharon's raspy laugh. Both of us turned around and saw that Tharon had reformed himself back into his "human" form, and was now just standing there.

"Well, well," he said advancing on us, "nowhere to run now." Tharon stuck out his hand and gestured at The Time Stone Gwen had in her hand. "Now hand me the stone, or else face the same punishment as your friends."

Instead of listening, Gwen instead drew her sword and got into a fighting stance. I drew Kit out too and got into what was probably the most pathetic fighting stance ever. Tharon laughed and said, "So, you think you can stand against me. I been trained in the art of sword fighting since I was eight."

"So was I," Gwen said narrowing her eyes. "Oh it's not you I'm concerned with my dear," Tharon said turning his eyes towards me, "but I suppose if this is the way you two both choose to die, I guess I will comply." And then magically Tharon made two shadow swords materialize out of thin air.

"Get ready," Gwen hissed at me.

"For what?" I asked.

There was a brief moment of pause as Tharon and Gwen both eyed each other before Gwen shouted, "NOW!"

Immediately Gwen and Tharon leaped for each other, catching me off guard. Both of their swords met and the two of them started swinging them around, battling each other. After my initial shock had worn off I jumped in to try and help Gwen, but Tharon used his other sword to block mine. I tried to counter with one of the moves Gwen had taught me but Tharon just blocked it again.

"How pathetic," Tharon laughed as he shot an energy blast directly at me which caused me to go flying backwards.

"Dad!" I heard Gwen yell. I groaned and rolled over as I tried to get back up, but the force of the blast had knocked the wind out of me making it impossible.

I laid there on the roof and watched as Gwen continued to battle for her life against Tharon. Both were equally good swordfighters, matched well against each other. Every time one threw a jab or tried to do a blow to the other person, the other person would simply block it. I looked over at the mountains and saw that the sky was growing brighter and I knew it wouldn't be that much longer that Gwen had to hold Tharon off. However, I could tell that the battle was taking its toll.

Gwen had started to sweat and each of her attacks seemed to have less and less power, and Tharon was starting to get frustrated that Gwen was keeping him from killing her. The fighting kept going on for a few more minutes, each person going back in forth in terms of attacks. Then finally Tharon had had enough.

Using his manipulation over shadows, Tharon made Gwen stumble for a second. During that time Tharon thrust his sword at Gwen managing to pierce her in the shoulders, causing Gwen to scream in pain. He then shot an energy blast at her, making Gwen go flying through the air.

"NOOOOO!" I screamed.

As I sat there and watched Gwen go flying backwards something happened. Time seemed to slow down again and the weariness and exhaustion I had was replaced by determination and pure rage. Immediately I jumped up and charged at Tharon. Just when I was a few feet away I brought my sword down on him. Tharon was lightning fast though and able to turn around and easily block my attack.

"Back again court jester?" Tharon said mockingly.

"You...Will...Pay," I said through gritted teeth.

Tharon laughed at my comment and behind him I heard Gwen scream, "Dad!" I looked behind him and saw that Gwen was hanging off the side of the roof, barely hanging on with her arm that wasn't wounded.

"You will join her," Tharon said menacingly. Hearing him say that only made me angrier than I already was.

I yelled in fury as I swung my sword at Tharon, however, he blocked my every swing. Each time Tharon laughed more and more and it was obvious he was enjoying my weak attempt to attack him. Swing after swing I tried to hit, but it proved to be useless. Tharon was just too good. Finally after several minutes of me fighting him, Tharon must have gotten bored because he changed things around and started attacking me. Immediately I drew my shield out to protect myself while Tharon used both his swords to send blow after blow to me.

As I tried to protect myself I wondered just how I could get the upper hand, but thankfully Gwen provided me with an idea.

"Dad, your feet!" I heard Gwen yell. I looked down at the ground and saw that Gwen had dropped her sword when Tharon hit her. A plan instantly popped into my head. I ducked and picked up Gwen's sword in my other hand which was difficult since it was a lot bigger than Kit, but after doing so I knew just what to do. I pounced.

I jumped back up and brought down Kit on Tharon. Tharon blocked it, but I used Gwen's sword to stab him. Tharon wasn't expecting me to use two swords, so Gwen's sword hit its mark. Tharon recoiled from the stab and I knew that I had him. I instantly went to work delivering blow after blow that Tharon desperately tried to block. With each attack I dealt my confidence and excitement intensified as I realized that I was winning. That was, until Tharon decided to play dirty again.

"ENOUGH!" Tharon shouted as he released another bolt of energy that sent me flying across the roof again. I tried to get up, but this time Tharon was through with toying with me. He pointed his sword directly at my face, "I've had enough of you, you idiot court jester. Now you shall pay!" Tharon lifted his sword to stab me and I closed my eyes as my short life flashed before them and I waited for the pain to start. To my relief, the pain never came.

Instead I heard a blood-curdling scream and I opened my eyes to see that Tharon's hand had a hole in it, like if something had burned right through it. I looked over at the mountains and saw that the sun was now peaking over the top of them. I sighed in relief as I realized I had done it. More and more of the sun peaked out from behind the mountains and more and more of Tharon's body caught on fire as he screamed in agony.

I saw him turn his eyes towards me and I knew that if he was going down, he was going to take me with him. Thinking quickly, I grabbed Kit and used it to reflect more of the light at him. Tharon reeled back in agony and his body began to glow bright white. I closed my eyes and turned my head away, listening to Tharon's screaming until suddenly the light died away and everything became quiet.

I opened my eyes and looked around. Tharon was nowhere to be seen. I took a second to catch my breath before I remembered Gwen. I turned around and saw that she was slipping. "Dad!" she screamed. Immediately I pushed myself up and jumped towards her, and just as Gwen let go of the roof I managed to grab her hand. Instead of saving her though, I overestimated my jump and I too was thrown over the side.

I grabbed hold of the edge of the roof with my other hand as Gwen and I dangled hundreds of feet above Morendale. I did my best not to look down as I desperately tried to hold onto the roof. Soon holding onto the roof while holding Gwen was proving impossible. My hand began to sweat and I felt myself slipping. I didn't know what to do. I started to panic. "I can't hold on," I yelled.

Then just when I was about to let go, another hand came out and grabbed me. I looked up and saw Tamina, a frustrated yet determined look on her face. "You...Are...Not...Going...To...Die...After...I...Came...All ...This...Way!" she said through gritted teeth as she used all her strength to pull both Gwen and I up.

Tamina managed to pull Gwen and I back onto the roof and once we were safely back on, all three of us collapsed from exhaustion. I took several deep breaths and as I did I saw not only Tamina, but Stewart, Leo, Rachael and Pipsqueak. Suddenly I was pulled into another bone-crushing hug by Gwen. "You were amazing Dad!" she screamed right into my ear.

I gritted my teeth at the volume but found myself not caring as I hugged Gwen back too. I looked over at everyone else and saw that everyone had smiling faces. All except Tamina who had an awkward expression on her face, like she was intruding on a private meeting.

I smiled and said, "Come on Mom, don't you want to meet your granddaughter." Upon hearing me say Mom again, Tamina burst into tears. She ran over and pulled both me and Gwen into the tightest hug ever, even tighter than Gwen's. I closed my eyes and enjoyed the moment as behind me I could hear Pipsqueak happily chirping as Leo said, "It's over. It's finally over."

Chapter 18

Goodbyes and New Beginnings

The afternoon sun hung high over Morendale as Leo, Tamina, Stewart and I waited out on the castle grounds for Gwen and Rachael. As we waited I looked over Morendale's village, with Pipsqueak on my shoulder chirping happily and occasionally nuzzling my cheek. After Tharon had been killed the people of Morendale went straight to work, using their incredible crafting skills and magic to repair the damage that had been done to the kingdom.

Within just a matter of hours both Morendale's castle and every building in the village had been repaired. Now when you looked at it you would've never known that a giant fire-breathing dragon had almost destroyed everything.

The door of the castle opened and Gwen and Rachael came strolling down the front steps towards us. Gwen had changed back into her old torn peach nightgown again since she would be leaving both her sword and her armor here in the past, and her entire right arm was in bandages. After the battle with Tharon, Gwen was taken straight to the infirmary so her arm could be treated and thanks to a quick swig of medicine with Heamed nectar her arm started to heal within a matter of hours.

"Are you ready?" Leo asked when the girls reached us. Gwen silently nodded and I could tell she was slightly depressed. I couldn't blame her. Our journey together might have been short, but after being through about half-a-dozen life-threatening situations, seeing Gwen leave made me feel sad. I looked down at The Time Stone in my hand. Leo had taken it after Tharon's defeat for safekeeping, but while I was in the infirmary with Gwen he asked to speak with me in private. He handed me the stone and said that since I was Gwen's father I should be the one to give it to her when the time came to send her back home. I was reluctant at first because the stone only reminded me about how Gwen was going back to her own time and that I wouldn't see her for a long, *long*, time, but after a little more persuasion from both Leo and Tamina, I finally gave in and agreed to be the one to give it to her.

I felt a hand on my shoulder and looked up to see Leo looking down at me, a sad look on his face too. "It's time," he said solemnly. I looked back down at the stone in my hand and hesitated for a second, then, very slowly, I stretched out my arm and opened my hand, revealing the stone to Gwen. Gwen slowly took it from me and held it tightly in her hand. After a moment of silence Gwen went around the group and started saying her goodbyes to everyone.

She first went up to Stewart and Leo and saluted them in respect. Leo and Stewart saluted her back. Next, Gwen went up to Tamina and, to my surprise, gave Tamina a small hug. Tamina was surprised at first, but after a moment she too hugged Gwen back.

"Bye Grandma," Gwen said. I snorted and suppressed a laugh as I thought about Tamina being old enough to be a grandma. Gwen then walked over to Rachael and both girls hesitated for a second before giving each other a large hug.

"I'm going to miss you," I heard Rachael say through small sniffles.

"Don't worry, we'll see each other again," Gwen said comfortably.

"Promise?" Rachael asked.

"Promise," Gwen answered. I couldn't help but smile at the scene. We hadn't been in Morendale all that long, but nonetheless, it was obvious that Gwen and Rachael were close.

Then finally, after Gwen and Rachael broke apart from their hug, Gwen made her way over to me. She stopped directly in front of me and there was a long awkward silence as we stared at each other, both of us unable to find the right words to say.

Eventually Gwen was the one to break the silence when she said, "Thanks, Dad. For everything." She then pulled me into another one of her bone-crushing hugs. At that point I couldn't care less how much they hurt, I just closed my eyes and enjoyed the moment. But that moment was soon broken when I started hearing a strange noise.

I opened my eyes and saw that Pipsqueak was cooing as he nuzzled Gwen's cheek like he usually did with mine. Gwen was laughing, completely ignoring the burn mark Pipsqueak was giving her. "I'm going to miss you too, little brother," she said.

I chuckled and said, "Well technically you're not born yet, so really that would mean he's your older brother."

Gwen laughed and said, "Yeah, I guess you're right."

We broke apart and Gwen started taking a few steps back. "Oh and one more thing," I said, "I want you to know, I'm grounding you when you get back."

The rest of the group laughed, but Gwen only shrugged her shoulders. "Well I say I got about twenty years for you to forget about this whole thing, so I'm not really *that* worried." I laughed at her statement and Gwen said, "And besides, I'm more worried about Mom."

I stopped laughing. "Wait, mom!" I asked dumbfounded. Both Gwen and Rachael broke out into a fit of giggles as I stared off into space, completely speechless.

"Goodbye, Dad," Gwen said.

I snapped back to reality and I saw Gwen waving goodbye. I brought my hand up and waved goodbye back. After a brief moment Gwen stretched her arm with The Time Stone in it out and closed her eyes and I could tell she was thinking hard. Then almost instantaneously, a bright blue and white light began to glow out of Gwen's hand and became bigger and bigger. The light eventually grew to engulf all of Gwen. Then, almost as soon as the light had appeared, the light was gone, and The Time Stone fell to the ground and lay on the soft grass. Gwen was gone.

Leo walked over and picked The Time Stone up. He then walked back over to me and placed the stone back into my hand. I looked down at the stone again and as I did I felt tears forming in my eyes. Tamina put a hand on my shoulders to comfort me. Without even

194

giving it a second thought I wrapped my arms around her and started crying. Gwen was gone. My daughter was gone and it was going to be years before I ever saw her again.

Tamina stroked my back and whispered soothingly, "It's ok, you did well, I am very proud of you." Hearing Tamina say that made me feel better and after a minute I calmed down and was able to dry my eyes. "Gwen is very lucky to have you," Tamina said smiling as we pulled away from each other, "and so am I." I couldn't help but smile as I thought about how much Tamina actually cared for me.

Behind me Leo said, "Well then, now that that's all settled, we still have one more thing to do. We have to get you three back home."

Compared to my journey *to* Morendale, my journey *from* Morendale was nothing. Literally nothing. Not one significant or exciting thing happened during our journey back home. That was probably because of what Leo did for us. Not only did Leo provide us with horses, but both he and Rachael said they would accompany us on our trip back. Even better than that, Leo ordered about a hundred soldiers to ride along with us for protection.

The journey started with us riding through the mountain pass and across The Wasteland. Most of the journey I spent talking with Rachael, getting to know her better. When our group passed the canyon with the rock monsters in it, we stopped for the night and continued on when the sun came up. When we reached the river where Gwen and I almost drowned, I wondered just how exactly we were going to get across, but I got my answer when Leo stuck his walking stick in the water and the river receded, making a pathway for all of us to cross. We then entered The Dark Forest, but thanks to the amount of guards we had, traveling through it was no trouble at all this time.

Finally after several days of traveling, I saw the edge of The Dark Forest and I knew that we were home. Our group rode out of

195

the forest and into the village. And I must say that was *truly* a sight to behold.

Tamina, Stewart and I went first, followed by Leo and Rachael, and then the guards of Morendale. It was midday so all the townspeople were out and about when we rode in and when they first saw us everything became dead silent. People stared at us as we passed, almost like they couldn't believe what they were seeing. Suddenly we heard the sound of a trumpet being blown and I knew that the Royal Guard was being alerted. We stopped and a few minutes later we saw Cornelius riding down to the village on his horse with several members of the Royal Guard right behind him.

As soon as he saw the three of us standing there he stopped dead in his tracks. After a moment of staring at us he slid off his horse and slowly approached. Tamina dismounted her horse too and walked up to her father and after a brief moment of silence both of them embraced each other in an emotional hug. When they broke apart Cornelius demanded to know what had happened, but before Tamina could answer Leo dismounted his horse and introduced himself.

"I think," Leo said turning around to face me, "we should let your court jester tell the story."

We all rode back to the castle and for the rest of the day I sat in the throne room and told my story. Almost everyone was there: all of the castle's staff, Cornelius, Lana, all the Royal Guard members. Every single person listened to me tell the story about me and my daughter. At first nobody believed my story but then I showed them Pipsqueak and everyone in the room was completely shocked by the tiny phoenix. After I had finished my story the room was absolutely speechless. When everyone finally did come around, Cornelius said something that made *me* absolutely speechless.

He said that due to my journey and showing courage in the face of danger, I would no longer be required to fulfill my duties as court jester. He told me that starting at the beginning of next week I would report to Stewart to start training as a member of the Royal Guard. I almost couldn't believe it. I was becoming a member of the

Royal Guard, just like I always wanted. Just like what Gwen had told me. Everyone in the room applauded me, Tamina being the loudest, and I couldn't help but blush.

Later that night another thing occurred that I thought would never happened. A party. And not a "Royal Celebration" kind of party, I mean an *actual* party. Everyone from the kingdom was there, and all of them were having a good time. I walked around the room and saw several of the guards from Morendale performing magic tricks to onlookers who clapped and cheered whenever they made fire erupt from their hands or shot off a firework. In another corner Pipsqueak was flying around and chirping happily as a group of small children laughed and tried to catch the tiny bird with their small hands. I smiled, finally glad to see that there was a party where everyone was having a great time.

"Excuse me," I heard a voice say behind me. I turned around and saw Rachael, wearing the same green dress that she had worn before. "May I have this dance," she said sticking her hand out.

"Yes," I said taking Rachael's arm and leading her out onto the dance floor where people were actually dancing. The band started playing a slow tune. Knowing what I was doing from dancing with Gwen, I took Rachael's hand, placed my other hand on her hip and started leading her in a waltz around the room.

As we danced, I saw Tamina and Stewart also dancing with each other and I couldn't help but smile as I remembered what Gwen had told me about the two of them. I also saw Leo and Cornelius up at the high table eating and talking to one another. Both of them looked up and smiled and saluted me with their drinks and I nodded back at them. I continued dancing with Rachael.

As she moved closer to me, I blushed a little in embarrassment, but I soon found myself not caring about it. I closed my eyes and simply enjoyed the dance. And as I did, I knew that Rachael, Tamina, Stewart, Leo, Cornelius, and everybody else, including me and my future daughter Gwen, were all going to live happily ever after.

The End!

About the Author

Jacob Sharpe is the author of The Tale of the Court Jester. Having written the book while attending college, Jacob graduated from Iowa State University and currently lives in Norwalk Iowa. To learn more about Jacob, visit his Website at www.jacob-sharpe.com

www.ingramcontent.com/pod-product-compliance
Lightning Source LLC
Chambersburg PA
CBHW031952130726
47905CB00003BA/763